DOUBLE A RANCH

A Montana Country Inn Romance Novel - Book 4

AMY RAFFERTY

© **Copyright 2022 Amy Rafferty — All rights reserved.**

This is a work of fiction. Names, characters, places, and incidents either are products of the author's imagination or are used fictitiously. Any similarity to actual events or locales or persons, living or dead, is entirely coincidental.

All rights reserved. No part of this publication may be reproduced, stored in, or introduced into a retrieval system, or transmitted, in any form, or by any means (electronic, mechanical, photocopying, recording, or otherwise) without the prior written permission of the copyright owner.

The author acknowledges the trademarked status and trademark owners of various products referenced in this work of fiction, which have been used without permission.

The publication / use of the trademarks is not authorized, associated with, or sponsored by the trademark owners.

Formatted by Author Services by Sarah

STAY UPDATED WITH ME

Thank you so much for purchasing or downloading my book! I am grateful to all my amazing readers.

To stay updated on all my latest books, newsletters, freebies and beautiful photos from the fabulous locations I write about, why not join my VIP group?

I will send you regular pictures of La Jolla Cove, San Diego and the Florida Gulf Beaches where I try to spend as much time as I can. I live in San Diego, my own 'Garden Of Eden' and I am in love with the sea and the beaches in the area. They inspire me to write lots of beachy mystery romance fiction to share with my awesome readers like you. To join me go to https://landing.mailerlite.com/webforms/landing/y6w2d2

You will be asked for your email. You also get a FREE BOOK whenever you sign-up!

FREE BOOK

To get your FREE copy of Cody Bay Inn Prequel - Nantucket Calling go to www.amazon.com/B0992NFTY1

CHARACTER LIST

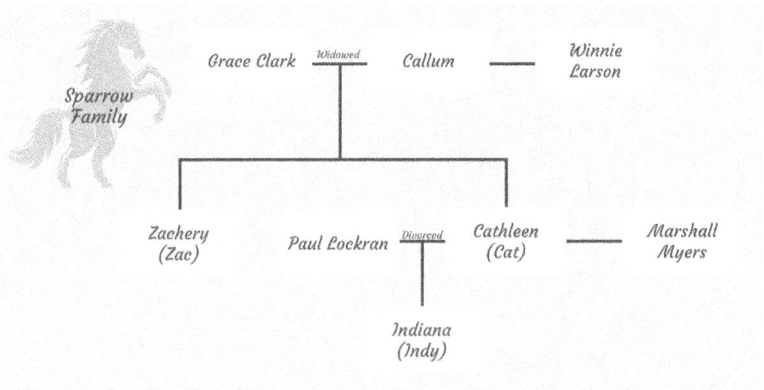

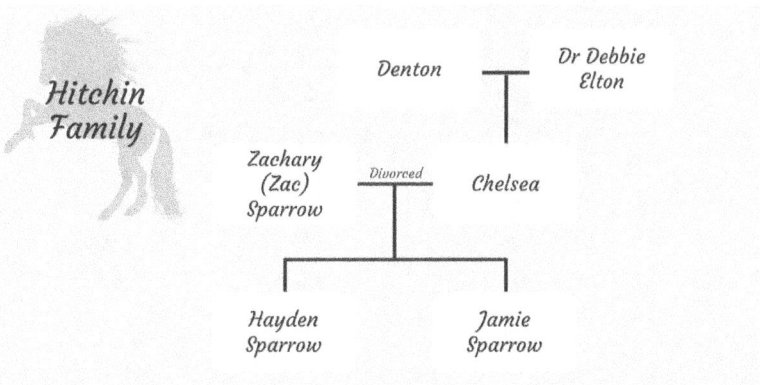

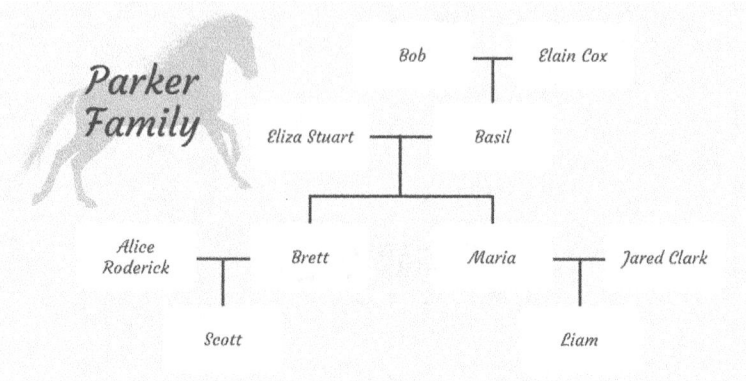

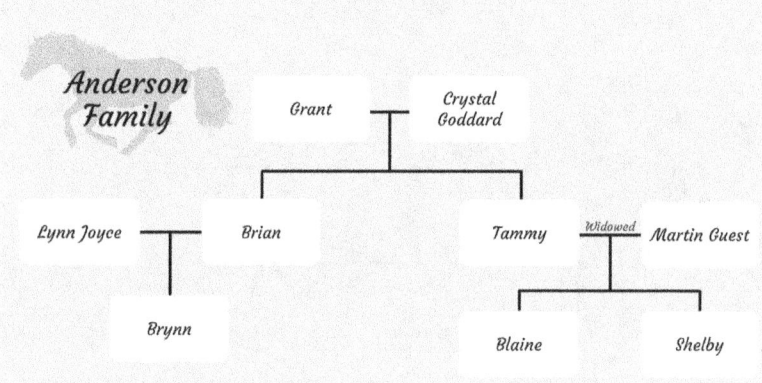

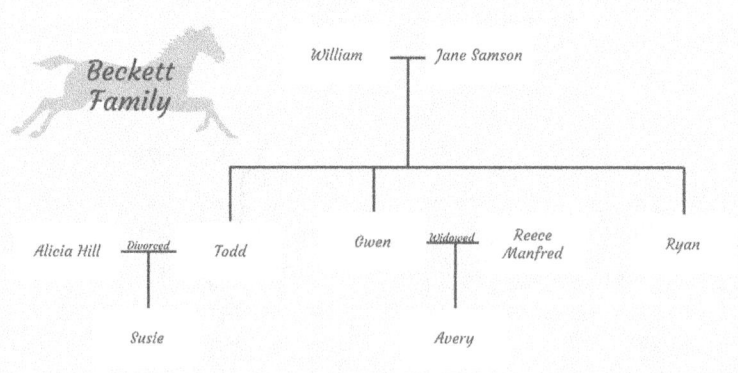

MAP OF THE RANCHES

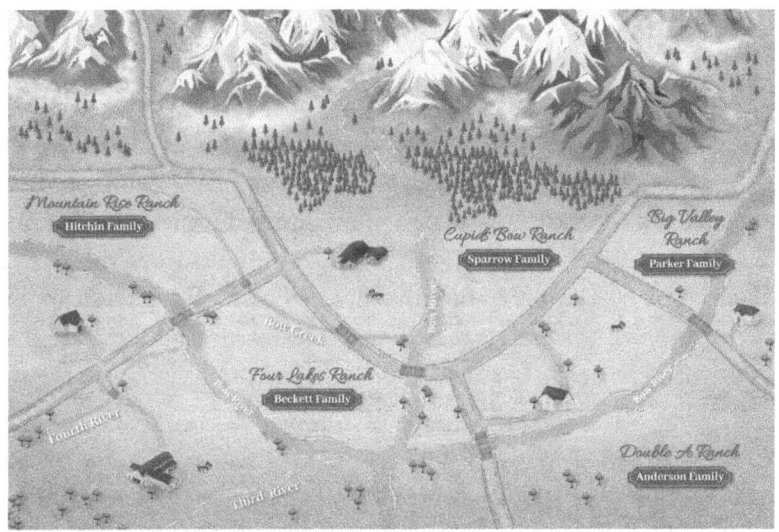

Chapter One

SOMETHING ENDS, SOMETHING NEW BEGINS - PART ONE

THREE YEARS AGO

Tammy Anderson-Guest's life was at a crossroads. She stood in her large corner office in Downtown Los Angeles and watched the rain pelt onto the window. Tammy could see people scurrying along the sidewalk below as they tried to get out of the rain. Tammy shivered and rubbed her upper arms. A grin spread across her pink lip-glossed lips as she thought how disgusted her older brother, Brian, would be with her if he could see her right now. She was shivering just by looking at the miserable rainy winter weather, which was warm compared to winters in her hometown in Montana.

Tammy had lived in Los Angeles for the past thirty-one years and had tried to only get back to Montana during the summer. She'd not gotten home as often as she should have, which was making this decision she had to make by tomorrow evening even harder for her. Martin, her husband of twenty-nine years, would understand and support her whichever choice she made. Tammy knew that, and she also knew he'd probably really love it if she decided to take this new opportunity that had been offered to her. Her intercom buzzed, pulling her from her thoughts.

Tammy walked over to her desk and answered it.

"Is Calvin here already?" Tammy asked her assistant, checking her wristwatch.

"No, Tammy," Brenda sounded apologetic. "He actually phoned to cancel because he's boarding an airplane to Bermuda."

"What the..." Tammy hissed and pinched the bridge of her nose. "Is he out of his mind?" She threw her hands in the air.

"I did warn him that now was not the time for him to go jetting off to yet another party scene," Brenda told Tammy. "What do you want me to do?"

"Call Angela and get her on the next flight to wherever Calvin Barlow is going," Tammy ordered. "She is to glue herself to his side and make Calvin very aware that this is his last chance. He is going to lose the contract with the studio if he gets one more strike."

"Will do," Brenda said. "Why don't you go home and surprise your husband? Didn't you tell me he had a few days off?"

"You know, Brenda, I think that is a wonderful idea," Tammy agreed with her. "I can discuss this new opportunity with him."

"Are you really thinking of putting off your early retirement for another three years?" Brenda asked her.

"Are you trying to get rid of me, Brenda?" Tammy laughed as she packed up her desk for the day.

"Oh, no," Brenda assured her. "I want you to take that job because I know where you go, I go, and I would *love* to spend the next three years in London."

"So would I!" Tammy admitted before clicking off the intercom and checking that she had everything before picking up her purse and walking out her office door. "You'll lock up?"

Tammy knew Brenda would.

"Of course." Brenda nodded. "Good luck, and text me right away to let me know when to start packing." She grinned.

Tammy shook her head at the eager young woman. Brenda had come to her as an intern fifteen years ago and worked her way to become Tammy's right-hand person. In fact, Tammy would be lost without Brenda, who was fifteen years younger than Tammy. She had also become one of Tammy's best friends and the only person he really trusted in Los Angeles.

"I will let you know as soon as I've discussed the deal with Martin and seen how he feels about putting off our retirement for another three years," Tammy promised.

"Normal people usually only retire in their late sixties, early seventies," Brenda pointed out. "You're not even fifty yet..."

"I'll be fifty in three months' time," Tammy reminded Brenda.

"But that's not old, that's middle-aged," Brenda said. "I know you and Martin want to jet-set all over the world for fun and not work. But even at fifty-three and fifty-five you can still do that and liven up your middle age."

"You're absolutely right," Tammy told her. "Besides, it's only me that won't be retired. Martin will still be able to start his early retirement."

"Yes, and in London!" Brenda said with a huge grin.

"I'd better go," Tammy said. "Before you twist my rubber arm even more and I march straight into Guy's office and accept the offer."

"I'm so glad I'm not married," Brenda said, shaking her head. "This is one of the reasons my marriage didn't work. I like to make snap decisions without having to consult someone else."

"No, you're no longer married because Simon was not a nice person," Tammy reminded her. "Now, I must go. I will call you later."

Tammy said goodbye and rushed to the elevators when she saw their doors opening.

On the way home, Tammy made Travis, her driver, stop at Martin's favorite seafood restaurant to pick up his favorite lobster dish. Her last stop before going home to the Bel Air mansion was to the liquor store to get a nice bottle of champagne. Martin loved a good bottle of bubbly, and it would be nice to celebrate whichever decision they made.

"Are you ready to head home now, Mrs. Anderson-Guest?" Travis looked at her in the mirror.

"I am, thank you, Travis," Tammy smiled. "I picked you up some of that shrimp you liked from the restaurant as well." She handed him the take-out bag.

"You spoil me, Mrs. Anderson-Guest," Travis thanked her and pulled out onto the road, heading for Bel Air.

When she got to her large sprawling mansion, Tammy thought it strange that no one was there to greet her at the front door. She frowned, taking off her soaked coat and hanging it on the rack near the front door. She asked Travis if he'd put the food in the kitchen. Tammy walked into the ground floor bathroom to get a towel to dry herself off before dismissing Travis for the day.

After not finding Martin in any of the ground floor rooms, Tammy went upstairs to their bedroom, but he was not there either. She frowned. That was strange. His phone was pinging from the house. He must be downstairs in the pool area. Martin loved lounging in the spa in the afternoons, so that's where he must be. Tammy quickly changed into a full-piece swimsuit and put a flowing caftan over it. She slipped on a comfortable pair of day slippers before heading down to the lower ground floor to find her husband.

She stopped at the kitchen to pick up the bottle of champagne she'd bought. When she got to the bar area, she quickly put the bottle on a bucket of ice and retrieved two flute glasses. Tammy's heart beat excitedly as she took the bucket and glasses into the pool area. She was sure Martin would agree to postpone their current plans because he, too, loved London. It was one of the first places they were going to visit when they'd formally retire. Martin was a popular talk show host on a show that had been on the air with excellent ratings for the past twenty-five years. His mother had been a well-known News presenter, and his younger sister, Amy, a famous actress.

Tammy was a PR manager to the stars and a partner in one of the biggest PR firms in Los Angeles. She's worked hard to get to where she was now, and she'd gotten to the top on her own, not riding on her husband's family's fame to do so. Tammy knew Martin was as proud of her achievements as she was of his. To celebrate her success, Martin had agreed to let her buy this house as well as the other four properties they owned. She was sure that Martin was going to want her to take the opportunity that had just been handed to her. Tammy's heart hammered like it still always did when she saw him. Even the part of her husband's head that she could see from around the wall surrounding the spa to separate it from the pool had that effect on her.

She grinned as she drew nearer, but before she could step out of her shoes to go join him, her heart seemed to stop. Tammy's eyes widened in surprise, and for a moment the world around her froze as Martin came into full view. Only Martin was not alone in their spa, and the person he was with had her lips locked to Martin's in a rather passionate kiss.

"Martin?" Tammy breathed when the world unfroze. The champagne bucket hit the tiled floor, sounding like a blast in the stillness of the room.

Martin seemed to move like lightning. He pushed the woman away so fast that she almost hit her head on the side of the spa. Then the poor woman got soaked in the tidal wave he caused by jumping out of the water.

"Tammy, what are you doing home so early?" Martin asked, grabbing the towel from the hook and glancing at the clock on the far wall. "You're not supposed to be home for another four hours."

"It's my home, and I can arrive here at whatever time I please!" Tammy heard herself say in a calm flat voice. The tone was similar to that she used when she had to iron out a difficult situation at work.

But Tammy was feeling anything but calm. She had to clench her fists at her side to stop herself from picking up the ice bucket and hurling it at his head. Tammy drew in a few deep breaths to keep herself steady and tried to contain the flames of anger burning inside of her.

"This is not what it looks like," Martin said, drying his feet off and stepping toward her.

Tammy took a few steps back, her eyes glancing down at the bucket lying on the floor surrounded by ice and broken glass. She wondered if she should warn him to be careful because he didn't have shoes on but then realized she no longer owned him anything. He had broken their vows, her heart, and their marriage. Tammy had told Martin right from the beginning of their relationship that the one thing she didn't tolerate was infidelity. Martin had assured her that she was the only woman he'd ever want in his life ever again.

When one of their friends' marriages had broken up because the one spouse had cheated, Martin had sided with the spouse that had cheated. He'd tried to get their friend that had been cheated on to work things out and go to couple's therapy with her husband.

Tammy had been quite surprised that Martin had done that. Especially after they'd both agreed that cheating was the one thing that would be the end of their relationship. Tammy had seen what had happened to her brother when his wife had cheated on him. She'd also seen what had happened to her grandmother when her grandfather had left her for his younger secretary. Tammy couldn't stand cheaters. She always wondered, if a person could cheat on another person with someone else, what other underhanded deeds could be involved in their lives?

"Tammy?" Martin's voice broke the veil her thoughts had put up to pull her from the situation she found herself in. "Please talk to me. Don't hide in your head like you do when you don't want to face something."

"You should deem yourself lucky at this particular moment that I prefer to retreat into my thoughts instead of clonking you on the head with a heavy ice bucket," Tammy told him. "Because right now, my heart wants me to pick it up and fling it at you while my mind wants me to back off and process this."

"Tammy, please, let's take a minute to calm down and then go talk about this," Martin suggested as if they'd just had an argument. "I'll get Hetty to make you some of your herbal tea."

"Where is Hetty?" Tammy's anger was getting harder to contain.

"Oh, that's right, I gave the staff the afternoon off." Martin shook his head and rolled his eyes.

"You'd best get out of the spa, Ursula," Tammy looked around Martin to the woman trying to hide away in the spa. "You're going to get even more wrinkled than you were before."

Tammy couldn't believe she'd just said that. It was not like her to say nasty things to anyone. It seemed her initial numbness over the shock of seeing her husband tangled in another woman's arms was starting to wear off, and her other darker emotions were taking over.

"Tammy!" Martin said, shocked at her outburst.

Tammy's brows shot up as she looked at him in amazement. Did he really just admonish her?

"This was nothing more than a silly slip-up and a misunderstanding!" Martin told her as Ursula wrapped one of Tammy's big fluffy towels around herself and started walking towards them.

"Excuse me?" Ursula, who was also the producer of Martin's show, hissed. "A silly slip-up?" She hissed, and her angry eyes flew towards Tammy's. "This *slip-up* has been going on right under your ignorant nose for the past five years." Her voice dripped with venom. "Not that you'd ever notice, though, because the beautiful, ex-cover girl, Tammy Anderson, never notices anyone in the background."

"What?" Tammy frowned, looking at the woman who was about ten years her junior but looked like she was five years older. Tammy put that down to the stress of the woman's job. "You're in my house, having a sordid affair with my husband, and you have the gall to accuse me of something like that when you hardly know me?"

"Oh, I know you!" Ursula spat. Her eyes blazed as she tried to step past Martin to face Tammy, but Martin held up his arm, stopping her. "Don't you dare try to stop me from having my say."

"I'm trying to stop you from cutting your feet to pieces on the glass on the floor," Martin said through clenched teeth. "I'm also trying to stop you from doing something as stupid, like attacking my wife in her own home."

"Oh, you mean this home that should be mine and our son's!" Ursula shouted in Martin's face.

Martin's shoulders tensed and his eyes narrowed, blazing with anger as he glared at Ursula, "I'm warning you not to say another word." His jaw was clenched, and a muscle ticked at its side as he stared Ursula down.

"What is she talking about, Martin?" Tammy felt a roaring start in her ears as shock wave blasts at Ursula's words started pounding through her. It felt like a tidal wave was hitting her.

Tammy's eyes widened as they searched Martin's face, looking for signs that the woman was just being spiteful and trying to hurt Tammy.

"Oh, you heard me," Ursula said spitefully. "I gave Martin something you couldn't give him. A child."

"Shut up, Ursula!" Martin barked. His voice was so full of anger that he'd made both Ursula and Tammy jump.

"Is this true, Martin?" Tammy somehow managed to find her voice through the confusion, anger, and hurt winding through her system.

"All you could offer him were those stupid orphaned Basset hounds." Ursula had to stick one more knife into Tammy's heart.

It was also the straw that broke through the swirling turmoil of emotions whirling inside of Tammy, letting the hot anger burning inside her spew out like lava from a long-dormant volcano.

"Where are my fur babies?" Tammy's eyes slit as she chose to ignore Ursula and look at Martin.

"I had to lock them up because they don't like Ursula,"

Martin told her, a frown creasing his brow as he looked at Tammy.

Tammy stood staring at Martin for a few seconds. Her eyes bore into his, searching for something that looked just a bit like regret, remorse. Even shame would do right now. But there was nothing. Martin was standing there as cool as cucumber with his mistress behind him and his wife in front of him. That's when Tammy realized he thought he was going to be able to talk his way out of this situation.

Something Ursula had said registered with her fogged brain, "Five years, Martin?" It was more a statement than a question. "That explains why you took Saul's side when he cheated on Wendy."

"What?" Martin looked at her, confused. "What have Wendy and Saul got to do with this?"

"Nothing," Tammy said, shaking her head. "You locked my babies up because your mistress doesn't like them?"

"They don't like her," Martin corrected, still wearing a confused frown as he tried to figure out what Tammy was up to.

"So, you locked up my babies in their own home because they were uncomfortable with you bringing your mistress into their domain?" Tammy's anger was growing by the minute.

Tammy could feel it spurring her on, changing her as it slowly took her over. Usually, she'd put a lid on it. Take a few steps back and calm herself down. But not this time. This time, Tammy retreated into the darkness and let the anger loose.

"I want you both out of my house," Tammy told him.

Her voice was emotionless and flat, belying the fire that she knew must've turned her eyes a deep shade of blue. Tammy's brother had said the only way he ever knew anger had taken over her was because her eyes turned a dark shade of blue and her voice became flat. She knew what Brian had meant by her voice. Tammy had heard it and couldn't believe it was hers.

"Tammy!" Martin said, trying to reason with her. "Please, baby, let's talk about this."

"You have two minutes to clear off my property before I call the police," Tammy warned him.

"You can't kick Martin out of his own house," Ursula piped up. "Tell her to get out, Martin."

"Ursula, shut up," Martin turned and hissed at her. "Just stop talking, okay?"

"This is your house, right?" Ursula's eyes narrowed.

"Well, Martin?" Tammy looked at him, a cold smile curling up the one side of her mouth. "Answer her."

"Tammy, please, let me just put her in an Uber, and then we can work this out." Martin looked at her. "You know I love you."

"Excuse me?" Ursula spat. "You said you had fallen out of love with her and, as soon as you could, you were leaving her." She gave him a shove. "We have a son together. He and I have been waiting for you to divorce her for five years!"

"I'm warning you, Ursula..." Martin glared at her. "Please, just go."

"No!" Ursula said. "This ends now." She turned and glared at Tammy. "You can keep this stupid mansion. I was only going to sell it anyway. I much preferred Martin's house in Malibu."

"You took her to Malibu?" Tammy's eyes widened in astonishment.

"Tammy," Martin was about to take a step towards her but glanced down at the border of glass shards that were separating them. "We were looking for a place to shoot a live morning show. That's all."

"So, you took her to *my* house in Malibu as well?" Tammy's voice shook as the anger started to turn into red hot rage. "Get out!"

Tammy pointed towards the door.

"Can we please just talk this through?" Martin pleaded.

"GET OUT!" Tammy's voice cracked through the room as the angry command tore from her throat.

"Is everything alright, Mrs–" Travis rushed into the room, stopping when he saw the scene in front of him.

"Could you please call Martin and his guest an Uber?" Tammy didn't bother to turn around.

"I'd be happy to take them," Travis offered.

Tammy spun around and Travis flinched at the look she gave him.

"Mr. Guest and his friend are not welcome to use any of my facilities, including my cars. Is that clear?" Tammy hissed. "And Travis," her eyes slit. "If I find you knew about this or drove them anywhere during the past five years, you, too, will be out on the street."

"I…" Travis shrunk back. "I swear I didn't," he assured her. "I only work for you."

"Leave the kid out of this," Martin told her. "He only ever drives you around."

"I thought I gave you a few minutes to leave my property?" Tammy turned and gave Martin an icy stare.

"I'd like to pack some of my clothes at least," Martin told her.

"I'll have them packed and shipped to you," Tammy told him and glanced at her wristwatch. "You have one minute to get clear off my property now."

Tammy stepped back and looked pointedly at the door.

Martin shook his head and started to walk to the door with an angry Ursula following him.

"Oh, and please leave my towels at the front door." Tammy looked pointedly at the towels Martin and Ursula had wrapped around them.

"Don't be spiteful, Tammy. It doesn't suit you." Martin pulled the towel off and purposely dumped it on the floor in front of Tammy.

"I'll see them out," Travis told Tammy and fled the room.

"The police have checked both the house in Malibu and the apartment in the city, and I have someone standing by in case Martin tries to go to your house in Santa Barbara," Brenda told Tammy as she shoved some more lobster into her mouth. "This is sooo good."

"I'm glad someone got to enjoy it," Tammy told Brenda. "Thank you for coming over."

"Of course," Brenda said. "I'm so sorry, Tam."

"How didn't I see it?" Tammy flopped down on the sofa next to the three Bassets that were lying on top of each other in their favorite spot.

"I guess he was just so good at hiding it," Brenda told her. "Are you not even going to talk to him before you see your lawyer in the morning?"

"We don't even know where he went," Tammy pointed out. "Not that it would make any difference." She frowned. "I expected something different."

"What do you mean?" Brenda curled her feet up on the sofa, wiping her mouth with a napkin.

"When I first caught them together, he was surprised to see me." Tammy's frown deepened. "But there was no shock or an *'uh-oh'*, an iota of guilt, or any sign of remorse whatsoever."

"Narcissists are like that," Brenda explained. "Their giant egos make them think they can work their way out of any situation."

"I guess you were always right about him." Tammy laughed. "He was an over-confident jerk after all."

"I said 'an over-confident narcissistic jerk,'" Brenda corrected her.

"Yes, you did." Tammy looked at Brenda. "You'd only met Martin a few times as well."

"He'd made a pass at me and then made it seem like I'd come on to him," Brenda reminded Tammy. "I nearly lost my job with you because of him."

"I thought he was sweet, arguing for you to keep your job," Tammy said softly. "I'm sorry, Brenda, I should've believed you."

"It's okay, I got to keep my job, and we became close friends." Brenda shrugged. "As far as I'm concerned, it's all water under the bridge. I knew one day he'd slip up. Karma always dishes out just desserts."

"Don't get mad at me, but I have to know," Tammy said. "Did you know he was having a long-term affair?"

"No," Brenda said honestly, shaking her head, before biting her lip and looking apologetically at Tammy. "But to be honest, I did have my suspicions."

"Oh?" Tammy frowned. "Why didn't you say anything?"

"We all have a blind spot, which is like that mysterious pain we can't quite pinpoint," Brenda explained. "Deep down we know what the pain is, but we don't want to face it in case it's malignant."

"Ah, so you think, subconsciously, I knew too?" Tammy guessed where Brenda was going with her explanation.

"Yup," Brenda confirmed. "We ignore the pain or just take stuff to make the symptoms go away because we know the cure would be to cut it out. No one wants that kind of pain or the scars it's going to leave."

"Why isn't there any?" Tammy patted April, the female Basset's head when it flopped onto her lap.

"Why wasn't there any what?" Brenda's brows creased.

"Pain!" Tammy looked at her. "Where is the pain?"

"I think you're still in shock and dealing with the anger," Brenda pointed out. "The full force of what happened has probably not really hit you yet."

"They have a child together!" Tammy shook her head and her eyes misted over.

That was something that hurt. The fact that Tammy couldn't have kids. It's not that she didn't want to, it was that she couldn't.

"Tammy, how do you know you were the one who couldn't have kids?" Brenda asked her.

"Because Martin went to be tested, and the doctors said he was perfectly fine," Tammy told her. "So, the problem was me."

"Did you get tested too?" Brenda asked her.

"Yes. The doctors told Martin it was me. I was away when the results came back." Tammy gave a shaky sigh as she tried to swallow the tears that had started to gather. "I guess that was my other hidden sore spot I didn't want to face. I couldn't give Martin the child he'd wanted."

"Tammy!" Brenda scooched forward on the sofa and took her hand. "No." She shook her head. "Don't ever say that. It's him who has let you down, and I'm sorry, you can hate me if you want to, but I think he's done this more than once during the course of your marriage."

"I want to be mad at you for saying that and for pointing out just how naive and blind I've been," Tammy swiped at the stray tear that had slid down her cheek. "But these have been the thoughts running through my head over these past few hours."

"I'm sorry, Tam." Brenda gave her hand a squeeze. "But you were not naive. You trusted the man you love. You supported him and were a good wife to him. You gave him the perfect marriage."

"Yes, but I couldn't give him the one thing he wanted; kids," Tammy pointed out. "I knew he wanted kids, but then, when I couldn't have any, he didn't want to adopt. He said that if we were not meant to have kids then we were meant to just have each other."

"Did he want you to get tested to see if you could maybe do IVF?" Brenda asked.

"No," Tammy told her. "Why are you harping on about my fertility test?"

"I'm not sure," Brenda said. "But something is bothering me about that."

"Why?"

"Look at this." Brenda leaned forward and picked up her phone. "This is Ursula's son."

"I really don't want to see this!" Tammy told her.

"I think you do," Brenda held the phone up in front of Tammy. "I'm not trying to be cruel, Tam."

"Oh!" Tammy took the phone and looked at the picture of Ursula and her son. "Is Ursula Hispanic?" She frowned. "Maybe her hair is dyed blonde?"

"I don't think she is," Brenda told Tammy. "Her hair has always been a mousy blonde."

Brenda flicked through Ursula's social media pages.

"She has blue eyes, and sandy hair with a Scottish surname." Brenda tilted her head as she looked at one of the pictures. "Her mother could be Hispanic. But this picture is tagged as her parents."

"They look English," Tammy said.

"Yes, and her mother's name is Beatrice Wellington," Brenda pointed out. "What if the child isn't Martin's after all?"

"It makes no difference." Tammy shrugged. "My marriage is officially over."

Chapter Two
SOMETHING ENDS, SOMETHING NEW BEGINS - PART TWO

THREE YEARS AGO – CONTINUED...

Tammy sat still, staring at the picture of Ursula's son Brenda was showing her.

"So, you think that the child isn't Martin's?" Tammy asked Brenda.

"I'm saying maybe if he was adopted, he might not be," Brenda suggested. "I wonder who Ursula was seeing before she met Martin?"

"Ursula started working at Martin's network about five and a half years ago." Tammy bit the side of her mouth as she remembered the first time she'd met the woman. "She joined just before Christmas, and I met her at the television network's annual Christmas ball. I remember because she'd brought Carlos from Channel One with her."

"Carlos Santiago?" Brenda's eyes widened. "*The* Carlos Santiago?"

"Yes," Tammy nodded. "Why?"

"You do know that his family is rumored to head up a Cartel in Mexico, right?" Brenda looked at her, wide-eyed.

"Those are only rumors because his father is some sort of powerful politician," Tammy corrected her.

"How do you think he got that position?" Brenda asked.

"Besides that," Tammy waved the Carlos subject off. "Are you trying to say that Ursula's son could be Carlos'?"

"That's exactly what I'm saying," Brenda confirmed. "What if all this time Martin was the one with the problem and that's why you could never have children?"

"I guess it really doesn't make any difference now." Tammy gave her a sad smile. "I'll be fifty in a few months' time. It's not like I'm going to be a mother anytime soon."

"No, but it will be one less thing you'll have to feel guilty about when you wonder what you could've done to have stopped Martin from having an affair," Brenda said softly. "Trust me, you might not be feeling it now, or even thinking about it. But those thoughts are going to come. You're going to start wanting to blame yourself for his betrayal."

"I guess," Tammy said. "But it's probably too late for me to find out now. I'm probably in some phase of menopause already."

"But we can find out what the real results of his tests were," Brenda suggested. "Or if he even got tested at all."

"I don't know," Tammy sighed and flopped her head back against the cushions. "I'm just tired right now. Tomorrow, I have to go and start the divorce proceedings."

"Do you want me to go with you?" Brenda offered.

"Would you?" Tammy turned her head to look at Brenda. "It would be good to have someone who'll remember everything. I'm afraid it may just be one of those days where everything just washes over me like a bad dream."

"Of course," Brenda said. "I know this isn't a good time to ask, but what are you going to do about taking over the new agency acquisition of our firm in London?"

"I'm going to take it," Tammy told her without hesitation. "I think three years in London is just what we need right now."

"I couldn't agree more," Brenda said. "I'm here for you every step of the way through this," she assured Tammy. "Just like you were for me when I went through my divorce two years ago."

"Thank you." Tammy squeezed Brenda's hand. "I think I'm going to go to bed now."

"I think I will do the same," Brenda said. She was staying over with Tammy.

"There should be everything you need in your favorite guest room." Tammy stood, and as she did so did her three dogs. "Do you want a dog?"

"You can give me Derby. He ends up scratching at the door in the early hours for me to let him in anyway." Brenda laughed.

"Yes, he does have a crush on you." Tammy smiled. "Okay then. I'll see you in the morning, and thanks for coming over at such short notice."

"Anytime." Brenda said.

Tammy said good night and went to one of the other spare rooms. There was no way she was going to go to the main bedroom that she'd shared with that traitorous Martin. As she climbed into bed after a shower and tended to her skin, Tammy made a note to call a realtor in the morning.

As she cuddled up next to two of her Bassets, her mind raced over which properties she was going to sell. If she was going to London for three years, there'd be no point keeping all of them. The only house she was going to keep was the one on the beach in Malibu. That was going to be her retirement house.

Tammy drifted off to sleep, her mind going over the events of the day. Her dreams were plagued with little bits of evidence that pointed to Martin having cheated on her their entire marriage. When she woke up the next morning, she was feeling even more tired than when she'd gone to bed the previous night. Tammy's mind was filled with all the little signs she'd known were there during her marriage; signs she'd chosen to ignore. Even Martin's younger sister, Amy had tried to warn her, but she'd just fobbed her off like she had done with Brenda.

Amy and Martin didn't get along. He'd been very mean to his sister when she'd had a breakdown and had to go to a wellness center. Tammy had often wondered what had actually happened to Amy. Martin had warned Tammy to never speak to Amy about it because it was a sensitive issue. Ever since then, Tammy hadn't seen Amy much, and when they did see Amy, she was shut off, reserved even. She hardly spoke to Martin at all. The one time she'd pulled Tammy aside was to warn her that Martin wasn't who Tammy thought he was and that she should watch her back with him.

Tammy had thought that was a rather strange thing for Amy to say about her brother. Tammy had put it down to Amy being mad at Martin for the part he'd played in forcing her to get help. Was there more to that story that Tammy had not seen as well? She made a mental note to find out more about Amy's alleged breakdown. Tammy shuddered as she realized just how she'd been manipulated and blinded by Martin over all these years. She shook her head to clear it and got up to shower and get ready for her day. Tammy had a long day ahead of her with a lot to do. All she could say was thank goodness for Brenda.

"Are you sure you want to do this?" Tammy's lawyer, Robert Goddard, asked her. "You don't want to try and iron things out with Martin first?"

"You and Brenda sound alike on that point," Tammy told him. "No, I don't want to talk it out with Martin. In fact, I never want that man to darken my door or life ever again."

"Tammy, you've done a complete three-hundred-and-sixty degree turn on how you feel about Martin in less than twenty-four hours," Robert pointed out. "It wasn't more than two days ago that you phoned me to ask me if you could amend your will. You wanted to make sure Martin was taken care of in the event of anything happening to you."

"We were supposed to be retiring together then and going on an adventure," Tammy reminded him. "Now I want him out of my will, my life, and I want to have no part of his."

"Fair enough," Robert said. "Let's get this amended right now, have you sign it, and then we can get down to the divorce."

"Thank you," Tammy said.

Once the will was sorted out and Tammy made sure everything she had would go to her niece, they started to discuss the divorce.

"Are you happy now that I made you make up your own prenup when Martin's mother was forcing you to sign the one she had drawn up for him?" Robert laughed. "She was so afraid you were going to steal their family fortunes." He sighed and looked at her with pride shining in his eyes. "I feel like a proud father when I look at you."

"That's because you're my mother's younger brother," Tammy pointed out. "And you stepped in as the role of a father figure when I moved to Los Angeles."

"Yes, I did." Robert's chest puffed up. "You were just a young greenhorn back then. But look at you know. Confident and successful beyond my wildest expectations. Now I'm the one worried about Martin Guest trying to take all your money."

"He won't," Tammy said confidently. "Because you won't let him. I take it that the prenup you had him sign is airtight?"

"Yes, especially if you can prove he was cheating on you," Robert said.

"I can, I saw it with my own two eyes," Tammy assured Robert.

"Yes, but is that the only evidence you have?" Robert looked at her with narrowed eyes.

"Actually, no, it's not," Brenda, who had not said a word up until this moment, told them. She pulled a flash disk from her pocket and handed it to Robert. "If Martin had brought Ursula around Tammy's house before yesterday, he'd been clever enough to erase the security feeds. He didn't have time this time around, so I pulled them for you."

"That will help if he tries to contest anything." Robert leaned over and took the disk from Brenda.

"Actually, I think he was in the pool room because he

thought there weren't any cameras in there," Tammy told them. "I had them installed a few weeks ago because I noticed that towels were going missing along with expensive alcohol."

"You thought your staff was stealing from you?" Robert asked her.

"I had hoped not," Tammy said. "I'd like to think I can trust them. Turns out I can."

"Every time Martin had Ursula over, he'd give the staff the morning or afternoon off," Tammy explained to Martin. "After questioning my staff this morning, they told me that over the past month that he's been home, it's been happening more and more."

"I thought he wasn't retiring for another few weeks?" Robert looked at Tammy, confused.

"He hasn't formally retired yet," Tammy said. "But he decided to take a couple of weeks off to see how the new host who is taking his place gets on."

"Or he was fired," Brenda shocked Tammy by saying. "I just hacked into the network's system, and his records show that his contract has been canceled."

"What?" Tammy and Robert said at once.

Brenda turned her tablet for them to see. "It says so right here."

"I can't use that," Robert told them. "I shouldn't even be seeing you do that!" His face flushed. Robert was a straight arrow that didn't like bending the corners. "But what I can do is try and find out what I can from the network."

"Thank you," Tammy said. "I'd appreciate that, and any information you can dig up about Ursula Duggal, the producer of Martin's talk show, would also be a help."

"I will," Robert promised. "In the meantime, I need you to avoid any talks with Martin without myself or at least Brenda present."

"That won't be a problem," Tammy assured Robert. "Brenda is leasing out her apartment, and I have offered her the guest room in my City Apartment."

"Oh?" Robert frowned. "Why are you selling your apartment?" He looked at Brenda.

"Because we're moving to London for three years," Brenda blurted out. "Tammy has been offered a fabulous position there."

"Really?" Robert looked at Tammy questioningly, and she nodded. "Wow, Tammy, that's amazing."

"Is this going to get in the way of my divorce?" Tammy asked. "I need to wrap this up as soon as possible because I'm selling all my property except the Malibu house."

"No, as per your prenup, that this is all yours," Robert assured her. "May I have the first offer on the Bel Air home?"

"Of course, Uncle Robert," Tammy said. "I was going to offer it to you. When I thought of selling it, you're the first person who sprung to mind. Although I'm not sure why you need such a big house."

"Grandchildren," Robert told her.

"Of course." Brenda rolled her eyes. "You have, what, three kids and twelve grandkids?"

"Number thirteen on the way," Robert said proudly.

"Isn't that a great-grandchild?" Tammy laughed.

"Still counts as a grandbaby," Robert insisted. "I'm sorry to rush this, but I have another meeting across town in thirty minutes."

"We're done for now," Tammy told him.

They said their goodbyes and left the offices. When they were walking towards the town car, a man with a hood walked rudely between Tammy and Brenda, nearly knocking them over.

"Hey, watch it, buddy!" Brenda hissed.

The man turned, and his cool, green eyes assessed them, making Tammy shiver. There was something familiar about him. He glared at them, pulled his hood further down over his face, and stalked off.

"How rude," Tammy said, rubbing her shoulder.

"I've seen him before, lurking outside the office," Brenda said. "I wonder what he's doing here?"

"It's not that far from our offices," Tammy pointed out. "He's probably just off to work."

"Just in case." Brenda shoved her hand into her purse and pulled out a taser. "You keep this with you."

"Good grief, Brenda. Put that away," Tammy said beneath her breath, quickly looking around to make sure no one was watching them. "You bring that thing into the office every day?"

Brenda nodded.

"How do you get it through security?" Tammy's face scrunched up before she shook her head. "Never mind, I don't want to know."

Brenda narrowed her eyes at Tammy. "I'm worried now."

Brenda put the taser back in her purse, and Tammy sighed in relief.

"Don't be Annie Oakley." Tammy looked at her watch. "The guy probably works in the same building or something. We have to get to the office. I have a meeting with Guy about the London deal in twenty minutes."

Tammy walked towards her car, where Travis was waiting to take them to the office.

"We leave in three weeks' time," Tammy told Brenda a few hours later, after she'd finished her meeting with the senior partner of the firm.

Brenda's eyes widened with excitement, and she jumped out of the chair she was sitting in Tammy's office to clap. Tammy shook her head and smiled, watching Brenda bounce around like a kangaroo.

"We have so much to do!" Brenda said wide-eyed, sitting back down and picking up her notepad.

"Yes, we do!" Tammy blew a stray hair out of her eye. "I will make some notes and send them through to you. Right now, I have a mess to help Angela clean up in the Bahamas."

"Oh no, what did Calvin do this time?" Brenda asked. Some of the excitement over London faded from her eyes.

"Oh, the usual, wrecked a hotel room. He broke into the hotel's bar when his mini bar ran out." Tammy rolled her eyes. "You know, the usual Calvin Barlow PR nightmare stuff."

"Let me know what you need," Brenda said, standing up and getting ready to leave. "I'll call Angela and get all the damage reports, etcetera."

"Thank you," Tammy said.

"Are you going to be okay with all this today?" Brenda stopped at the door and looked at Tammy worriedly. "You haven't so much as thrown a vase, stuck a knitting needle into one of Martin's photos or even shed a tear."

"I guess I'm still processing it all and trying to make sense of it in my head," Tammy said truthfully. "I'm sure all the rest will come."

"Well, I'm here when you need me." Brenda turned and left the office, pulling the door closed behind her.

Tammy sat staring at the closed door. It was the first time since she'd caught Martin with Ursula in their spa pool that she'd been completely alone. When she'd eventually gotten Martin and Ursula out of her house, Travis had been there, and the rest of her household staff had come back. Then Brenda arrived after Tammy had called her. She'd been so tired that when she'd gotten into bed she was still going through the motions and still a bit numb.

Her phone dinged. Tammy looked at the message from Robert. He'd already got the preliminary divorce documents ready for her to go over. Tammy closed her messages and her eyes fell on the background photo on her phone. It was of her, Martin, and the three Basset hounds. Tammy's hands began to shake as she stared into Martin's eyes. He had a relaxed smile on his face with his arm possessively around her shoulders. In all the time she'd been with Martin, she'd only ever felt safe with him. But now, when she looked at this picture it was like she was seeing him for the first time. That wasn't a protective pose. It was a possessive one.

How could she not have seen that before? Martin had been overly possessive of Tammy. He'd also been the one that had stopped them from visiting her brother in Montana as often as she'd wanted to.

"Oh, my word," Tammy hissed. "Martin was as possessive and controlling as both Brenda and his sister, Amy, had said he was."

Tammy's jaw clenched. She squeezed her eyes shut and shook her head.

How on earth could I have been so naïve? How have I been living with blinders on when it came to Martin for all these years?

She dropped her head into her hands and rubbed her forehead with her fingers.

"Good grief, Tammy," Tammy berated herself softly. "How could you have been so dumb?"

Her intercom buzzed. Tammy dropped her arms onto her desk and stared at it for a few seconds before it buzzed again. This time it went buzz, buzz, buzz, as Brenda was obviously getting impatient with Tammy's lack of an answer.

Tammy hit the button. "Yes?"

Tammy wasn't really in the mood to talk to anyone right now. She felt like curling up in a little ball and hiding away forever. How stupid everyone must've thought she was—because they all obviously saw what Martin was like. They had tried to warn her, and she'd just laughed them all off as if they were crazy. Her Martin was a good, loving husband. He brought her flowers and chocolates on a regular basis. Took her on date nights at least twice a week where they'd wine and dine, and he'd treat her like a princess.

But now, Tammy knew those were all guilty offerings from him to cover up his infidelity and stop her from realizing what a true controlling, narcissistic pig he really was! Anger spurted through her. It was like a hot blazing bowling ball knocking down the last of the tight control on her emotions.

"Are you okay?" Brenda sounded hesitant.

"I'm fine," Tammy snapped and immediately felt bad.

It wasn't Brenda's fault. She had tried to warn Tammy so many times. Then a thought struck her. Brenda was the one who suggested she go home and surprise Martin yesterday. Had she known?

"Did you know that Martin would be home with her yesterday?" Tammy asked before she could stop herself. *Uh, oh.* Before her brain was in gear, Tammy had engaged her mouth and spewed out a terrible accusation. "I'm sorry!" She said quickly.

"It's okay," Brenda said, sounding a little hurt. "For the record, no, I did not know Martin would have the audacity to bring another woman into your home."

"I know." Tammy sighed. "I'm sorry Brenda, I guess I just hit one of those grief stages."

"I'd say you're jumping all over that grief scale with your emotions," Brenda gave a soft laugh.

"Did you have something to tell me?" Tammy asked.

"Oh, yes," Brenda said. "I have something to show you. Can I bring it in?"

"Sure," Tammy said, letting go of the button and sitting back in her chair, trying to get a grip on the emotions toiling around inside her right now like a force five tornado.

Brenda burst through the door to Tammy's office with a document in her hand, kicking the door closed behind her.

"I had a friend from the network where Martin works give me some interesting information," Brenda said. Her eyes sparkled with excitement like they always did when she was onto something. "She had a *lot* to say about Martin, and then sent me a copy of Martin's actual termination documents."

"Termination?" Tammy's brow creased into a confused frown. "Why would they terminate the number one talk show host? I mean, his father owned the network, didn't he?"

"That is probably the only reason Martin Guest wasn't terminated years ago." Brenda pulled out the chair in front of Tammy's desk and sat down.

"What is all that?" Tammy looked at the documents as if they were a snake about to strike out and bit her.

"They are copies of Martin's personnel file." Brenda flipped through the large document in front of her. "You must see all the harassment charges that have been filed against Martin over the years."

"I really don't think I want to see them," Tammy told Brenda. She was feeling that horrible shockwave type of feeling she had when she'd seen Martin in the spa with Ursula again. "How stupid everyone must think I was."

Tammy pushed her chair away from her desk, stood up, and stared out the window. It was still raining, and the gloomy sky echoed the feeling inside her. While the raindrops splattering against the window were the tears, she wished she could curl up and weep. But what good would tears do? They were about as useful right now as the anger, pain, and other dark feelings whirling around inside of her. Tammy was better than some petty, blinded woman that had been misled by a lying, cheating, husband.

She was a successful woman who'd worked hard to get to the top of her career. Tammy had cleaned up so many messes made by her clients in similar positions over the years. Heck, Tammy had cleaned up some rather hair-raising messes her clients had found themselves in over the years. She wasn't someone who broke easily. Tammy was born and raised in Montana. She'd faced down wild untamable horses. Tammy had even roped and subdued her fair share of raging bulls. So no, she would not let some lying, cheating, misleading soon-to-be ex-husband break her or make her lower herself to his standards.

Tammy's momma, pappa, and nanna had raised her to pick herself up, dust herself off, and get right back on that horse after a fall. She smiled, thinking of what her nanna would say.

"Girlie, do ya have any broken bones?" Tammy would test her arms and legs then shake her head. "Then, little missy, what are ya waiting for? Get right back up on that beast and show him who's really boss here."

"Tammy?" Brenda's voice broke through Tammy's musing. "Do you want to go home for the rest of the day?" She asked softly. "I can hold down the fort here."

Tammy took a deep breath to calm the raging storm inside her. *I've not broken bones, nor am I bleeding. I'm picking myself up, dusting myself off, and I'm going to show the world I'm the boss of my life, no one else!* Martin Guest would soon be out of her life for good and she would put him behind. He would be like that bad memory and shelved with her life's lessons learned.

Love was not her strong point obviously, and she no longer had time for it. Tammy was a planner and she'd planned her life out right up to her retirement. But plans were just plans until they were implemented. That bit of her life's plan had not yet been implemented and would just need a bit of adjustment. That's exactly what Tammy would do. Adjust her plans. She turned and sighed.

"I don't want to go after Martin," Tammy told Brenda. "I would rather put him and his whole sordid life behind me as quickly as I can so I can start a new chapter of my life."

"Wow!" Brenda looked at her, amazed. "You know that you are allowed to get angry, to cry and to wallow in your pain for a while?"

"I'm not a wallowing type of person," Tammy pointed out. "I'm more of the 'sweep it all up and throw it away,' type of person."

"You spent twenty-nine years with this man," Brenda said. "You have every right to go after him with a pickaxe if you want to."

"What's that going to get me?" Tammy shrugged. "It's not going to change what happened or who he is." She sat back down. "What it does is make me look petty and weak."

"I would say it'd make you human," Brenda told her. "But I can see why you would take the high road and I admire that about you."

"I'm not sure how to take that," Tammy said. "But I'm going to take it as a compliment."

"That is how it was meant." Brenda smiled.

"Keep the information you've gathered about Martin," Tammy suggested. "You never know, I may need it sometime."

"Sure," Brenda said.

"You and I have a lot to do in the next couple of weeks to get ready to move to London for three years." Tammy pushed all thoughts of Martin and her broken life aside. There was plenty of time to reminisce when she was retired. "Let's not let anything spoil our UK adventure."

Tammy sat back and watched Brenda leave her office. When the door closed, she looked at it as a symbolic sign. Something had ended, but she was about to begin a new life with new, amended plans for her future. Tammy decided to concentrate on the positive instead of the negative and darkness the previous day had brought. She turned and looked out the window to see the sun trying to peek through the dark rain clouds.

"Yup, the light always finds a way to break through the darkness." Tammy smiled as a song from the musical Annie suddenly popped into her head, and she started to hum.

Chapter Three
THE AVALANCHE

SIX MONTHS AGO

Tammy was furious. It had been three years! Three years and that arrogant jerk still hadn't signed the divorce papers. Yet he'd agreed to the terms and hadn't contested anything in it. He'd just never signed them. Tammy had arrived back from the UK three days ago and had been settling into her Malibu house nestled right on the beach. She was getting ready to go and get some takeout from a sushi bar when Robert had phoned her.

It was not the phone call she was expecting from her uncle either. A few months after Tammy and Brenda had left for the UK, Robert had had a heart attack and was forced into early retirement. He'd put one of the junior partners in his firm on her divorce. Tammy knew that this mess she was now in was no one else's fault but her own. She should have kept on top of things back in Los Angeles. But Tammy had been so busy establishing herself and realigning the acquired company with the American one, that she'd dropped the ball. She'd let some of her business back home slide into her to-do pile that kept being pushed aside for more urgent things.

Tammy rubbed her temples as she stood staring at the ocean calmly lapping the shore and soothing her frazzled nerves with its sounds. She couldn't wait for summer to come so she could take her deck chair, a good book, and go sit on the sand to soak up the sun.

Tammy also really missed Brenda! She was so happy her dear friend had found such a great guy in the UK. Tammy had even become a guardian to their daughter, whom Tammy had the honor of meeting three weeks before she came back to the States. Still, she really, really missed Brenda.

Not only was Brenda Tammy's best friend in Los Angeles, but she'd been the best assistant anyone could wish to have. Brenda was on the ball. She could anticipate Tammy's every move and had an answer for everything. Tammy hadn't even realized just how much she'd relied on Brenda to sort out her everyday life until she'd handed in her resignation. It wasn't a surprise. Tammy had known it was coming the day Brenda announced she was pregnant. They'd discussed what would happen, especially because Tammy was moving back to Los Angeles. Brenda had even tried to talk Tammy into moving to England.

Brenda's new husband was also the man Tammy was training to take over her firm's London office, so Brenda really didn't need to work anymore. Andy, her husband, was more than capable of providing a life for her and their child. Tammy smiled, looking at her phone. Brenda had been the first person she'd wanted to call after Robert had dropped a bombshell on her head. Tammy wasn't a vindictive person, and she never wished any harm on anyone, but she was so glad that the lawyer that had been assigned to her case had been fired. Apparently, her case wasn't the only one the man had messed up or dropped the ball on. That still didn't help her case because she was still married to Martin. But that wasn't her only problem.

Tammy looked at the stack of bills a courier from Robert's offices had just delivered to her. Martin hadn't bothered to change his address. By the looks of some of the accounts, he had opened in the past three years he'd had no intention to either. Martin knew Tammy had sold her Bel Air house to her Uncle Robert and that she no longer owned it, but he kept listing it as his place of residence when opening one account after another. Just how many clothing accounts or store accounts did a person need? They weren't just average accounts either; they were all at high-end stores where he'd run up thousands of dollars in debt to each one of them.

The worst thing about the accounts was that there were two store cards for each account with the one in her name. So, Ursula, or whoever Martin was with now, was using credit cards in her name. As far as Tammy knew that was fraud, and she could prove she had nothing to do with these accounts. She wasn't even in the country when they were opened. Tammy and Martin were also legally separated, awaiting their divorce to be finalized. All Tammy needed now was for Uncle Robert to send through all the papers proving they were separated, as she'd already signed her part of the divorce. It was all dated and legally stamped by a judge as well.

Martin Guest may have been able to avoid all of Uncle Robert's firm's attempts to get him to sign the divorce papers. But he would not avoid Tammy. Enough was enough, and if he didn't want her to have him arrested for fraud, he'd freaking well sign these papers. Three years was long enough for him to draw this out and use her good name for his gain. As far as Uncle Robert had been able to find out, Martin had found a new show that his network was keen to produce. All Martin needed to do was find some investors who would be interested in financing the production. That seemed strange to Tammy. Why wouldn't the network that Martin's family owned want to sponsor the show themselves?

Tammy shook her head. She really didn't care, so she wasn't going to waste her time pondering over her estranged husband's affairs. Tammy wanted to kick back and put her early retirement plans into action. She was turning fifty-three in a few months' time and that would be her official retirement day even though she was unofficially retired right now. The firm had planned some big send-off party for her and wanted to have an official day. That was sweet, and it gave Tammy time to finally plan out what she was going to do. She hadn't had the time when she was in England.

What she really didn't want to be doing after only just landing back in the States was hunting down Martin Guest.

Her phone beeped and she picked it up. It was another message from her uncle. Martin was in Aspen on a skiing trip with some potential investors.

"Great!" Tammy hissed and flopped onto the sofa. "I've barely gotten over my jet lag and I'm going to have to go on a skiing trip."

At least the flight was only about an hour and a half to Colorado. Once again, the first thing Tammy wanted to do was call Brenda to book some flights.

"Come on, Tammy, you used to do all these things on your own before Brenda came along," Tammy picked up her tablet. "I'm sure you can book your own flights and accommodation."

Tammy was about to book her flight when she realized she needed the divorce papers first. So, she picked up her phone and dialed Robert.

"Hi, Tammy," Robert answered his phone after the third ring. "Did you get the information I sent you about Martin?"

"Hello, and yes I did, thank you," Tammy said. "I was about to book a flight to Aspen when I realized I need the divorce documents."

"You'll have to get them authenticated, Tammy," Robert told her. "Why don't I come with you?"

"I can't ask you to do that, Uncle Robert," Tammy told him. "You've had bypass surgery."

"That was years ago, Tammy." Robert laughed. "Besides, I could use a break and I love Aspen at this time of year."

"Well, it would be nice to have some company," Tammy admitted. "You get the papers ready, and I'll book the tickets."

"Great, I'll have them ready before close of business today,"

Robert told her. "I can be at the airport first thing in the morning."

"I'll get us the first flight out," Tammy told him.

"That was a rather bumpy ride!" Robert laughed as the taxi made its way to the ski resort.

"I have to agree it was not the smoothest flight I've ever had," Tammy said. "The pilot did say there was bad weather that we flew through."

"Let's hope it doesn't hit here before we're back in Los Angeles tomorrow." Robert looked out of the window. "Although, judging by the darkening sky, I'd say we may want to make sure we can keep our accommodation for a few days."

"Lovely!" Tammy sighed. "All I wanted to do was relax in my beach house with a good glass of wine and put together my retirement agenda."

"You have a retirement agenda?" Robert looked at his niece, surprised. "I'm nearly eighty and I'm looking for a way to stay at work."

"Yes, but, Uncle Robert, mom said you've been a workaholic since you were a child," Tammy remembered what her mother used to say about her younger brother.

"I did like to keep busy," Robert admitted. "That year I had to take it easy after that heart operation nearly did kill me. Especially with your Aunt Emily fussing about me like a busy bee all the time."

"I'll never understand how workaholics found time to get together like the two of you did." Tammy laughed.

"Oh, your Aunt was in her element," Robert told Tammy. "She could multi-task away, running her budding clothing line empire while planning all our pre-wedding parties, the wedding, and the honeymoon."

"I can imagine," Tammy said.

The cab slowed down as they neared the town. There was a police barricade up, redirecting traffic. The main street was lined with emergency vehicles.

"What on earth is going on here?" Robert leaned forward to look out the front window.

"I'm not too sure," the taxi driver said. "Let me radio in and find out if my company knows anything."

"Thank you," Robert tried to crane his neck to get a better view as a helicopter flew overhead. "Whatever is going on, it seems really serious."

A feeling of dread suddenly gripped Tammy's heart for some reason. Her chest started to feel tight as if someone was kneeling on it, and she was finding it hard to breathe.

"Tammy?" Robert's eyes widened as he turned and looked at her. "Are you okay?"

"I don't ..." Tammy swallowed and tried to suck air into her burning lungs. "I don't know."

"You're having a panic attack." Robert sprang into action and grabbed the brown paper bag the car had in case a passenger got sick. He put it over Tammy's mouth as she started to hyperventilate. "Breathe in and out into the bag as normally as you can."

"There's been an avalanche," the taxi driver told them. "The road is backed up and they are not letting cars through at the moment. My company is calling your hotel to see if they will let you in."

"Thank you, kind sir," Robert told the man while he helped Tammy calm down. "Are you feeling better?"

"I'm not sure," Tammy said honestly. "This weird icy cold feeling of dread just suddenly hit me out of nowhere, and I felt as if I was suffocating. Like I was trapped and running out of air."

"It's your nerves, my dear," Robert assured her. "You've been through so much, and you haven't seen Martin since the day you kicked him out, so it all probably just hit you."

"You're right," Tammy said, putting the paper bag over her mouth once again.

But something told her that was not the reason she'd suddenly felt this way. There was something else that she could not put her finger on, and a deep sadness fell over her heart.

Tears started to burn her eyes, and Tammy quickly squeezed them shut and swallowed down the lump gagging her throat.

What on earth is wrong with me? Tammy wondered. *Is Uncle Robert right and all those emotions I didn't shed three years ago suddenly burst out?* But that reason didn't feel right to Tammy. This was something else. It was a feeling she knew she'd experienced before. Her eyes widened when she remembered, the last time she'd felt like this she'd been nineteen and her father had died in a freak accident on the ranch.

"No, no, no," Tammy said, her hands shaking as she pulled out her phone.

"What's wrong, Tammy?" Robert asked her.

"It's Brian," Tammy blurted. "Somethings wrong with Brian."

"Why would you say that?" Robert's eyes widened.

"I can just feel it," Tammy dialed her brother Brian's number.

There was no answer. Tammy tried his wife's phone. Again, there was no answer. Finally, she tried her niece's phone and on the fourth ring, a strange woman answered.

"Hello?" The woman said. "Who is this?"

"I think the question is who are you?" Tammy's brows furrowed as the feeling of dread squeezed her heart a little tighter. "Why are you answering my nine-year-old niece's phone?"

"I'm sorry. I'm Janice Curt, I'm an EMT with the mountain rescue team in Aspen," the woman explained, making shock waves start to throb through Tammy. She knew, even before Janice could say any more, that the news she was about to tell Tammy was not good. "I'm sorry to tell you this, but your niece and her parents were involved in an avalanche on the slopes."

"No!" Tammy's eyes widened and her breathing once again became labored as she turned her head towards the flashing lights cluttering up the town's main street. "Are you sure it's them?" She asked stupidly "They're in Montana."

"Yes, I'm sure it's them," Janice answered. "May I ask where you are?"

"I'm here," was all Tammy could think to say.

"Here?" Tammy could hear the confusion in the EMT's voice. "Sorry, do you mean in Aspen?"

"Yes, we've just arrived and are at the end of the main street," Tammy's mind was reeling.

She thought if she kept Janice talking then maybe nothing bad had happened to her brother and his family. Tammy knew that was a stupid thought and that she was probably just panicking. She was just thinking the worst.

"Tammy, what is going on?" Robert asked her.

"I'm on the phone with an EMT," Tammy told him. She heard her voice come out of her mouth, but it sounded like it didn't belong to her. It was too squeaky and high-pitched. "Do you want to say hello?" *Did I really just say that?*

Tammy handed the phone to Robert feeling as if she was moving in slow motion inside a terrible dream.

"Okay..." Robert gave his niece a sideways glance as he took her phone.

"Hello?" a woman's voice came from the receiver. "Miss? Miss are you there?"

"Hello, this is Robert Goddard, I'm Tammy Anderson's Uncle." Robert kept a worried eye on Tammy who was staring at him like she was in a trance. "Who am I speaking to and what has my niece so spooked?"

Janice once again explained who she was. Tammy could hear her voice through the phone even though Robert had it pressed to his ear. She heard Janice tell Robert about the avalanche. That they'd recovered most of the injured and were now finishing off sweeping for bodies. Tammy knew without Robert having to confirm it that her brother was not one of the survivors before Janice told Robert that her brother and his wife didn't make it.

"You can go through to your hotel," the driver who'd been on the phone and missed what was going on in the back turned to tell them. "I can help you with your luggage if you like?"

"Yes," Tammy turned and looked blankly at the man. "That would be good. Thank you."

Before Robert could say anything, Tammy climbed out of the

taxi. The cold air wrapped around her, but Tammy was too numb to feel it or realize she didn't have her coat or gloves on. Janice had told Robert that Brynn was badly injured, but she would survive. However, neither her mother nor father had made it.

Brynn needs me. That was the only thought ticking through Tammy's mind as she stalked off into the foray of chaos in the main street.

Tammy didn't hear Robert calling her as he and the taxi driver rushed after her with their luggage. Tammy was focused on finding her niece that she now knew was somewhere in the myriad of flashing lights and numerous emergency workers. Her laser focus made her push through them all looking for where the survivors had been taken. Her mind couldn't focus on anything else right now. Tammy knew if it did, she'd crumble, and she didn't know if she'd ever be able to get back up again.

"This another wild horse, Tammy," Tammy murmured to herself. "Stare it down, keep strong, don't let fear in. Brynn needs you to be strong right now."

Tammy swallowed down the burning lump that was getting bigger in her throat with every step she took. Her mind reeled with questions, so much so she nearly never heard the faint voice calling her name. Tammy stopped dead in her tracks, frowning as she spun around.

"Amy?" Tammy gasped, spotting her on a gurney.

"Tammy!" Amy Guest, Martin's younger sister, called out to her again.

Tammy ran to her side. "Amy, what are you doing here?"

"Brynn!" Amy said weakly, slurring her words. "I tried to save her!" Her eyes welled up tears.

Blood was smeared over Amy's swollen bruised face. She could hardly understand what she was saying. Her bottom lip was so puffed up. Both her arms and one of her legs were in splints.

"Where is Brynn?" Tammy asked Amy.

"In the …" before Tammy could answer her eyes rolled back in her head and she started spasming.

"I need help here!" Tammy looked around shouting. "Someone please..."

A man ran up to where Amy was. He had a stethoscope around his neck.

"Sorry, could you please step aside?" The man, who Tammy presumed was a doctor, gently pulled Tammy to one side and stepped in to help Amy.

"Sorry, are you Tammy Anderson?" A woman's voice said from her side.

Tammy didn't turn her head to look at the woman. She stood staring in horror as the doctor worked on Amy. All she could do was nod.

"I'm Janice, we spoke on the phone," Janice said gently. "Your niece is this way."

Janice took Tammy by the arm and led her a few paces to the right. Tammy kept her eyes on Amy the whole time Janice moved her along.

"Aunt Tammy?" A small voice grabbed her attention.

Tammy's head shot around to see Brynn lying beneath a blanket. Her young face and her clothes were stained with blood.

"Brynn!" Tammy rushed to her side. "Oh my gosh, Brynn."

Tammy's eyes scanned Brynn's body from head to toe. She wanted to reach out and pull the scared nine-year-old girl into her arms, but she didn't know where Brynn was hurt.

"Can I hug her?" Tammy's voice was raw with the emotions she was trying so hard to keep down.

"Yes, just be careful around her left wrist and ribs," Janice warned Tammy. "And don't squeeze her too tight."

Janice hadn't finished her sentence before Tammy bent down and Brynn threw her arms around Tammy's neck.

"Don't leave me, please!" Brynn whispered into her ear. "Please, stay with me."

"Always, superstar, always," Tammy said, kissing Brynn's hair. "I'm not going anywhere."

"We have to move her now," Janice told Tammy.

"Tammy!" Robert called, sounding out of breath. "I've been looking for you."

"Uncle Robert!" Brynn looked when Tammy gently loosened herself from Brynn's grip.

"Hey, superstar," Robert's eyes were misty as he stared down at her before bending and kissing her brow.

"Aunt Tammy's staying with me," Brynn told Robert.

"Yes, she is," Robert confirmed. "I'll be right behind the ambulance."

"Okay," Brynn said softly.

"I'm sorry, sir," Janice said politely, "but we have to take her now."

"I'm coming with!" Tammy insisted.

"Of course," Janice said.

Brynn was wheeled to an ambulance Tammy climbed in on once they'd settled Brynn.

"Robert, please go see if Amy is okay!" Tammy told him.

"Amy Guest?" Robert looked confused. "I'll go find her."

Janice told Robert where he could find Amy before telling Tammy that Amy was now stable and about to be transported to the same hospital that Brynn was.

Robert blew a kiss at Brynn before turning to go look for Amy.

"Aunt Tammy," Brynn said, her eyes getting drowsy. "Aunt Amy saved me."

"She did?" Tammy looked at her, surprised. "When you're both better you're going to have to tell me what happened."

Brynn nodded and lay back.

"Try to stay awake, sweetheart," Janice said softly to Brynn as the ambulance took off.

THREE WEEKS LATER

Tammy pulled up outside the UM Upper Chesapeake Medical Center. Her niece, Brynn, and sister-in-law, Amy, were both being released today after three weeks in hospital care. As soon as she could, Tammy had Brynn and Amy taken by medical air transport to LA. She was still in a state of shock over the avalanche that had taken her brother, sister-in-law, and estranged husband's lives. Amy, Martin's younger sister, had also been in Aspen on the slopes. Thank goodness Amy had been there because she was the one who'd saved Brynn's life.

Amy's quick thinking and reflexes had pulled Brynn and herself out of the major slide by pulling them into a deep crevice in the rocks. They'd had to be dug out, but they were nearer to the bottom of the mountain. The dogs had found them within moments of the rescue crew arriving. Tammy was still in the dark about what her brother and his family or Amy were doing in Aspen. Amy had mentioned that Ursula Duggal, Martin's girlfriend, was also in Aspen, but her whereabouts were still unknown. The hotel in Aspen where Martin and Ursula were staying said that she'd checked out the morning of the accident. Ursula hadn't been on the slopes with Martin. She'd left Aspen hours before the avalanche, but there was no record of her taking a flight home to LA or any transportation. There wasn't even a record of her hiring a taxi to take her home. The rental car Martin had hired was still at the hotel.

Robert was still trying to track Ursula down. They had been unable to wait for Ursula to decide about Martin's funeral, so Tammy had arranged and paid for it all. There was a big turnout for his funeral that Tammy, as the host, had to attend. She represented Martin's only living family members as Amy was still in the hospital. Even though they'd been estranged for years it had still saddened her. Tammy couldn't believe they were all gone. Her brother, his wife, and Martin. All taken out in the same afternoon.

Tammy had arranged for her brother Brian and his wife,

Lynn's, bodies to be flown back to Montana. It still weighed heavily on Tammy's heart that she was not able to attend Brian's funeral. Tammy had done as much of the preparation for it as she could, but she had to rely on their long-time housekeeper, Constance, to do all the rest, including hosting the day. Constance did tell her, however, that her brother's best friend had helped her with everything. She was pleased that Constance had helped and had tried her best to ignore the fact that a man she despised had overseen her brother's funeral.

That must've pleased her brother's best friend to no end. Having something else to throw in her face if ever they had the misfortune of meeting ever again. But Tammy didn't have time to ponder on that horrible man. Her niece and Amy couldn't travel; they were still confined in the hospital. As Brynn's guardian Tammy had to be there to make any medical decisions that may need to be made. Besides, there was no way she was going to leave an injured, frightened, and grieving nine-year-old alone in a strange place. Constance had understood that and assured Tammy she was making the right choice.

As soon as they could all travel again, they'd have a small family memorial for Brian and Lynn. One that only Tammy, Brynn, and Constance would be at. That would enable both Brynn and Tammy to finally feel that Brian and Lynn were put to rest. Maybe when she was home for a few weeks, Brynn would have Constance to lean on for a while. Then Tammy would be able to let herself grieve for her loss. Each day, she got a little stronger, but the pain was always hovering above her heart waiting to be properly let in so it could tear into her soul.

Tammy shook her bleak thoughts off as she ran into the hospital. She didn't want to miss the doctors who were looking after both Brynn and Amy. They had a whole lot of care instructions and follow-up visits to heap onto her when she got there. Tammy looked at her watch. She was nice and early, which meant she could maybe grab a coffee. Tammy hadn't had time to get a cup that morning. She'd been rushing around making sure all the final arrangements for Brynn and Amy were put into place at her Malibu home.

Tammy had organized for Brynn and Amy to be in a private room together. They both seemed to be relieved that someone was with them. Tammy had found out the first night the two of them got moved to the ward that they both didn't like the dark. She'd bought a night light to leave in the room, one that projected soft stars onto the roof. Brynn had said it reminded her of all the stars in the sky back home in Montana. Tammy sighed as she remembered that conversation. It had nearly broken her, and it had made Tammy feel homesick for Montana. Something she hadn't felt in many years.

The pull for her home in Montana had begun when she'd had only three months left in the UK. Tammy had been feeling homesick, but she was surprised to find that when she dreamed of going home it was to Montana, not Malibu or LA. After that, the feeling of longing for the wide-open space, fresh country air, and a sky with billions of stars kept tugging at her heart. Now she wished she'd followed that feeling and gone straight home to Montana. Maybe then Brian and Lynn would still be alive. Tammy was still not sure what Brian and Lynn were doing in Aspen at the same time as Martin. As soon as Amy was settled, and Brynn was occupied elsewhere with the au pair Tammy had hired to help her with Brynn, she'd make sure Amy explained it all to Tammy.

Before Tammy could get to the ward to say hello before grabbing a coffee, she was stopped by one of the hospital's office staff.

"Mrs. Anderson-Guest," the woman called to her. "Could I please have a word with you?"

"Yes, of course," Tammy said, walking back toward the woman. "What is this about?"

Tammy was starting to feel disappointed that she was going to be told that she couldn't take either Brynn or Amy home today.

"It's about the hospital bill," the woman said, looking a little uncomfortable.

"I don't understand?" Tammy's brows furrowed.

"Could you please follow me into this waiting room? We'll have a bit more privacy," the woman gave Tammy a small smile.

"Sure." Tammy followed the woman into the room wondering what the heck the problem with Brynn's hospital bill was.

Tammy had paid the entire bill already and put down a hefty deposit when Brynn was brought in. In fact, Tammy had paid a deposit for both Brynn and Amy and covered the cost of the room. All Amy paid for were her medical procedures and various doctors.

"I've paid Brynn's bill in full," Tammy assured the woman. "I made sure there were no extra costs before I came here to fetch her today."

"Your bill is fine, Mrs. Anderson-Guest ..." the woman assured Tammy.

"Please, it's Tammy or Miss. Anderson," Tammy told the woman. "I've been separated and I filed for a divorce from my late husband three years ago. I no longer use his last name."

"Sorry, and noted," the woman said. "But it's not your bill I need to talk to you about. It's Amy Guest's."

"If Amy hasn't paid or her health insurance hasn't paid, I'm sure once she's out it'll get sorted," Tammy tilted her head. "I know there were some costs for the storage of my late husband's body as well, which Amy will cover. I can speak to her if you like?"

"No, no," the woman said. "The doctors don't want Miss. Guest worried. I'm afraid the Guest's health insurance lapsed some time ago. Her credit cards have also all been declined."

"What?" Tammy stared at the woman, dumbfounded. "How can that be?" She took the bills the woman handed her. "Amy is worth a small fortune, as is her family."

"I'm sorry, Mrs.... I mean Miss. Anderson, but nothing we've tried for payment has gone through." The woman looked embarrassed. "I feel awful having to put this on you, but you are still listed as Miss. Guest's next of kin and Mr. Guest's wife."

"Fine, I'll take care of them," Tammy said. Tammy fiddled in her purse and pulled out her black card. "Here, put it all on there."

"Would you follow me?" The woman stood up and led Tammy out of the room.

They walked down the hall towards an admin section. Tammy looked at her watch impatiently. She now only had about ten minutes before the doctors were meeting her. So much for grabbing a quick coffee. As she followed the woman into the office Tammy wondered what the heck was going on with Amy's money and health insurance. She knew Martin and Amy both had insurance. Tammy had taken care of it when she and Martin were still together. She had to ask Robert to look into this for her.

What else had Martin and Amy let lapse or get out of control in the past three years that had all Amy's cards being declined? Tammy sighed as she used her card to pay off Amy and Martin's outstanding medical bills. She didn't have a chance to fully examine the alarmingly large bill either. She shoved them and the receipts in her purse, thanked the woman, then rushed to go meet the doctors so she could take Amy and Brynn home.

Chapter Four
A DIFFERENT KIND OF AVALANCHE

FOUR MONTHS LATER

Tammy was furious! She couldn't believe the audacity of Martin's girlfriend. The woman who'd wrecked their marriage three years ago had sent her a lawyer's letter suing her for back child support. She was also demanding money from Martin's half of their estate. Tammy could not believe what she was reading. She'd gone straight to Robert to sort the mess out as there was no way Tammy was paying for Child support. Especially not all that back child support Ursula was trying to claim. Besides, Martin had no estate at the time of his death.

The letter had come after Ursula had been served an eviction notice to leave the house that she and Martin had been living in due to a lack of mortgage payments. Tammy had received one shock after another as Martin's mountain of bills started arriving for her as his wife because Martin had not signed the divorce papers by the time of his death. The house Martin and Ursula had bought had her name on the documents, but it wasn't even her signature on that page. Once again, Tammy wasn't even in the United States when these documents were signed. Robert was trying to get it all sorted out for her, but the bank wanted to attach all Tammy's assets because of the house, cars, and credit card bills. Both Martin's cars had already been repossessed. All the cell phones in Martin's name had been shut off due to lack of payments. The next thing to be shut off was the utilities if the bills weren't paid by the end of next week. By the looks of things, Martin had hardly paid for utilities over the past two years he'd lived in his big fancy house.

Tammy wasn't a heartless person, and she didn't want Ursula's child to suffer, but there was no way she was paying off the house, utilities, and cars. Nor was she paying maintenance or child support to Ursula. Tammy hadn't liked what she'd done, but she ordered a paternity test from the child after Robert had dug up some interesting information about Martin. He was sure Ursula's child wasn't Martin's. If that was the case and there were no legal adoption or guardian papers drawn up, Tammy didn't have to pay Ursula anything.

She was just dumbfounded that she may have to pay if the child was Martin's. How did that happen? Ursula was having an affair with Tammy's husband before they were estranged. She was the reason the marriage had ended. Tammy had all the proof on video with the times and dates which Robert was in possession of. There was also a prenup that Martin had signed, protecting Tammy's money and assets. But California was a no-blame state.

If Robert couldn't get Tammy out of the bank mess with the houses and cars, she was going to have to pay for them and then sell them as well as everything in the house. Before Ursula was served notice on the house, Robert had an assessor go around to take stock of everything in it. So, there was an itemized list, but Tammy really wasn't interested in any of the things inside Martin's house. There was nothing of value in it anyway. Any expensive paintings, household items, or jewelry of any value Martin may have had he'd sold, apparently. All Tammy wanted was to put this mess behind her and move on, build her new life with Brynn as well as Amy, who Tammy had also kind of inherited with Martin's death. After all, Amy was the closest person Tammy had to a sister and had always been on Tammy's side.

But Tammy also owed Amy Brynn's life. How do you ever repay a debt like that? Amy was also no leech, she'd gone and sold all her apartments, houses, and valuable items, and she was about to sell her jewelry and heirlooms when Tammy found out what she was doing. Tammy had stopped her selling any more things and insisted that Amy put all the money she'd made in a bank or invest so she could start again or start a nest egg.

It wasn't Amy's fault that Martin had done this to himself. Both Tammy and Amy had been in shock that Martin had somehow managed to drain Amy's trust fund. When he'd had Amy committed to a facility, because he insisted she'd had a breakdown, he'd got signing power of her estate. That included all her bank accounts as well.

Amy had finally told Tammy why Martin was in Aspen with Tammy's brother. He'd wanted Brian to invest in his show for the network that his family once owned. Tammy and Amy had found out that Martin had sold the network, as well as Amy's half, years ago. Amy had been under the assumption all these years that her share of the network's profits went into her trust account. They had actually gone into Martin's pocket until he'd sold the network, and Amy hadn't seen a penny of that money either. Amy had been none the wiser that the network no longer belonged to her family.

The biggest shock of all for Tammy had come two days before Ursula's letter. Some not very nice private security men had arrived at Tammy's door demanding money. Apparently, Ursula had sent them to Tammy as she was Martin's legal wife. Her first thought had been to buckle and pay the money as soon as possible. Tammy didn't have any experience dealing with these types of men. Well, not directly. She had people who did this if any of Tammy's clients got into this type of trouble. Luckily, Tammy also knew the protocol for dealing with thugs like them. She'd immediately called Robert and told the men to please wait in the car until her lawyer arrived. The men had gotten rather pushy, but Tammy had hired security a few weeks ago when Brynn thought she was being watched on the beach. Not long after that, Amy also reported she was being watched.

The man the agency had sent was not someone anyone would pick on in a hurry. But the man had proven that he had a soft side by the way he helped and looked after Brynn. Both Amy and Brynn felt safe with their new security detail. And on the day those thugs had arrived at her door, Tammy had been so glad she had hired him. The thugs soon backed off and went to wait for her in their car. It didn't take Robert that long to get to her house as he'd been en route to discuss a way out of this mess Martin had left her in. Robert spoke directly to the thugs' boss and told him they were willing to pay, but he'd have to sign a contract and hand over a valid receipt. There would also be a contract stating that once this debt was paid in full, they would never darken Tammy's door again. The boss agreed – all he wanted was his money. He was a businessman, after all, and told Robert he was not in the habit of terrorizing single women and children.

Tammy was getting more and more worried each day, though. Her nest egg was starting to get lower and lower while trying to sort Martin's mess out. Tammy's phone rang and she nearly jumped out of her skin; she'd been so deep in thought. She'd been standing in her living room in Malibu, staring out at the beach where Amy, Brynn, and Jude, the security detail, were walking on the sand. Amy had only just gotten all her casts off and Brynn had the pins in her leg replaced a week ago. So, Jude was watching them carefully and so were Tammy's three basset hounds.

Turns out Jude was studying to be a doctor when he'd enlisted in the army, but after five tours and seeing what he'd seen, he could no longer stand the sight of blood. So, he'd gone into private security instead. Tammy thought it was a bonus that he'd know what to do in an emergency.

Tammy's phone was still buzzing. She answered it just before it clicked off. It was Robert. He wanted her to meet him in his office this afternoon. Tammy had told him she just needed to get Amy and Brynn sorted out and make sure Jude knew she'd be gone for a while. Brynn seemed to be adjusting to life in Malibu, but Tammy had seen the pain as well as the longing for her home shining in the young girl's eyes; eyes that were so much like Tammy's brother's that every time she looked at Brynn, she saw Brian. She'd promised Brynn that as soon as the doctor had given her a clean bill of health, they'd visit Montana. If Tammy couldn't get this mess of Martin's sorted out and had to pay off all those bills, she might have to sell her Malibu house, then move home to Montana.

That now-familiar homesick pull towards Montana tugged at Tammy's heart. Every time Tammy thought about having to sell her Malibu house and move to Montana, a warmth crept over her. Tammy felt a calmness as well, like she'd finally be able to breathe again, when she thought about it. Maybe it was time to go back home. That was the thought going through Tammy as she was heading to her car to go meet Robert. It wasn't fair of Tammy to keep Brynn away from her friends, her school, and the home she'd grown up in. A home that was now Tammy's and would one day be Brynn's. She made a mental note to discuss the option with Robert, then Brynn and Amy. Tammy wasn't sure if Amy would even consider moving to Montana. But it may just be the fresh start Amy needed as well. Excitement pumped through Tammy's veins, and her heart felt lighter than it had in months.

Tammy's head was once again reeling as she stared at the medical reports in front of her. When she'd gotten to Robert's office, he hadn't wasted any time telling her what he'd dug up about hers and Martin's fertility tests they'd had when trying to have a child. It was all getting a little too much for Tammy. She felt like her chest was being squeezed as she found it hard to breathe.

"Are you okay, honey?" Robert's gentle voice reached out to her.

"I don't know," Tammy said honestly. "I feel like I've been caught in an avalanche and am being swept away in this sea of debt, lies, and betrayal."

"I know," Roberts said, sympathetically. "We now have all the evidence we need that Ursula's son is not Martin's."

"I feel awful for her," Tammy looked at Robert. "Now that we've agreed it's best for me to pay off the bank, I think we can give Ursula a bit of any profit made on the house. And please, can you get a car back for her? Sell the second one."

"Your heart is too big, Tammy," Robert told her. "I just hope she doesn't try to come back at you once she's worked her way through any money you give her."

"Make sure she signs an air-tight contract forbidding any other contact with me or anyone I know," Tammy instructed Robert. "She can also keep whatever furniture items she needs from the house."

"I will let her lawyers know and send them a copy of the paternity test," Robert said. "With your permission, I'd also like to send a copy of Martin's fertility test."

"Go ahead," Tammy told him. "I've decided I'm going to talk to Brynn and Amy tonight about moving to Montana."

"You're thinking of going home?" Robert looked at her in surprise.

"I am," Tammy admitted. "I've actually been thinking about home for a long time now. It's not fair of me to keep Brynn away from her home. She needs familiarity and stability right now."

"It's not even been four months since Brian and Lynn's death." Robert looked at her sympathetically. "Kids are hardy and bounce back a lot quicker than adults."

"Yes, but I'd rather she did it where she feels comfortable," Tammy said. "I'll discuss it with both Brynn and Amy. If Amy wants to stay in LA I will need you to help her with accommodation please, Robert."

"Of course." Robert nodded. "Are you selling your beach house?" His eyes lit up.

"No, I think I might just keep it and rent it out for a while," Tammy told him. "You don't know anyone looking for a beach house, do you?"

"As a matter of fact, I do," Robert smiled. "My eldest daughter and her husband want to downscale now that their kids are all grown. They are looking for a house in Malibu with beachfront access like yours."

"Well, if they like it and we decide to move, maybe they can lease with an option to buy once Brynn and I have decided what we're going to do," Tammy suggested.

"I think they would jump at that kind of offer," Robert assured her. "Will you let me know when you've decided?"

"You will be the first to know," Tammy promised him.

Tammy glanced at the medical records in her hand one more time before plopping them on Robert's heavy oak desk.

"You should go have yourself tested again," Robert told her. "You never know, you may just be able to have children."

"I'm nearly fifty-three, Uncle Robert." Tammy always reverted to calling him Uncle Robert when she was shocked or exasperated by him. "There is no way I would even think of having children now, even if I could."

"Women in their fifties are having babies, Tammy," Robert pointed out. "So don't rule it out."

"Uncle Robert, I don't even have a boyfriend, let alone a husband." Tammy laughed. "So, I don't think kids are on the table for me. Besides, I have my three fur babies, a nine-year-old girl, and a forty-eight-year-old woman to take care of now."

"Fine." Robert sighed. "As soon as we get any valid sales on Martin's house, I'll let you know and then we can discuss what a fair percentage for Ursula should be." He looked at her, shaking his head. "You could still get her arrested for fraudulently presenting herself as you."

"What would that do for me?" Tammy asked. "All it will do is leave her child without a mother and a father. He'd end up in a state home and be shoved into the foster care system. I don't want the child's life ruined because of Ursula and Martin's stupidity."

"You really do have a big heart." Robert gave her a proud smile. "I will be sure to let her lawyer know. I'll also make it clear that we'll be keeping everything on file should Ursula try to break the terms of the agreement we're having drawn up."

"Thank you." Tammy reached over the desk and patted his large hand fondly. "I don't know how I would've gotten through all this these past almost four months without you."

"Oh, you're a very capable young woman." Robert's eyes were glowing with admiration and pride as he stared at her. "I'm sure you'd have muddled your way through it all."

"That is very sweet of you to say, Uncle Robert," Tammy's voice was suddenly gruff with emotion.

"What are you going to do now that your retirement nest egg has been so badly depleted?" Robert looked at her with concern in his eyes. "You know if you need anything I'm always here."

"I do know, and I appreciate that so much, Uncle Robert," Tammy told him with a warm smile. "But I think my best option is to go home to Montana. It looks like that's the way fate is pushing me anyway."

"I think it will be really good for you and Brynn to go home," Robert assured her. "Maybe your aunt and I will take a trip there in the near future as well. Your mother loved Montana so much."

"You're always welcome, Uncle Robert, you know that." Tammy sat back in the chair. "Is there anything else I need to know?"

"No, we've covered everything," Robert told her. "I'll get all the paperwork drawn up for Ursula's lawyers and I will also take any meetings they may want. You just need to sign this form giving me full permission to act on your behalf should they try to demand anything else."

"Of course," Tammy said, leaning forward and signing the form. "I think she's gotten more than she should out of this. Oh, I would like you to set up a trust fund for her son though. I want you to manage it and make sure Ursula never knows about it or gets her hand on it, please."

"I will keep an eye on them both as well," Robert promised "Because I'm sure that's the next thing you're going to ask me to do."

"Like I said, why should that child suffer? It's not his fault, he is the innocent victim in all this." Tammy's eyes misted over suddenly as she thought of Martin. "I'm sorry." She sniffed and took the tissue Robert handed her. "I just suddenly got a little overwhelmed."

"Honey, you need to go home and have a good cry. As far as I know, you've not let yourself grieve even for a moment." Robert's eyes darkened with worry as they stared into hers.

"And how am I supposed to do that?" Tammy furiously fought to control the emotions once again trying to burst out of her chest. "I have a lot of things to get sorted out and people to take care of. Brynn needs me to be strong and help her through the loss of her parents. I know what that feels like."

Tammy felt her eyes sting and the back of her throat was starting to ache. But Tammy knew if she did start crying, she wasn't sure she'd be able to stop. What good would she be to anyone if she became a weepy wreck, unable to think straight? No, she was the captain steering her crew through a very bad emotional storm. While she was quivering inside, she had to hold on, be positive, and get them through this. Tammy had been through a lot of heartache and pain in her lifetime. She had learned how to weather the storm and this time she had others that needed her to help them through it.

"Tammy?" Robert's soft voice broke through her thoughts.

"Sorry, I was just thinking about everything I needed to do if I was going to move back to Montana," Tammy lied.

"It's okay, I understand." Robert leaned forward with his arms on his desk. "I asked you if you wanted me to keep you updated on the child?"

"Actually, I would like that," Tammy said. "I know it's not my place to judge anyone's parenting style. But Ursula left her son alone with a housekeeper while she jetted off to Aspen. I do worry about him."

"Leave it with me." Robert jotted some notes onto a notepad. "If you're serious about renting out your Malibu home I'll speak to my daughter."

"I am," Tammy nodded. "It'll be nice to know my cousin is living there and not some stranger. If they are serious about wanting to buy, I may just sell it to them in the near future."

"Trust me, if you do want to sell, I'm sure they will jump at it," Robert told her.

"Could I ask if it's not too much trouble if you could sort the lease out for me as well?" Tammy started gathering her things and getting ready to leave. "I will tell you our plans as soon as I've discussed it with Brynn and Amy."

"I can do that for you." Robert stood up when Tammy did.

Robert walked her to the office door, where he gave her a hug and a kiss on her forehead. Tammy said her goodbyes and left his office. When she was driving home, she passed a Lexus car dealer and saw the latest model SUV in the showroom window. Tammy didn't know what made her do it, but she pulled into the dealership. Within an hour, she'd found herself the proud new owner of the luxury version of the latest LX model. Tammy told the salesperson that she'd let them know where she wanted the car delivered. He assured Tammy that if she wanted it delivered to the Billings airport ready for her to collect it, wouldn't be a problem.

By the time Tammy drove into Malibu and meandered towards her house alongside the sparkling Pacific Ocean, a peaceful calm had washed over her. On the drive from LA to Malibu, she'd made up her mind that she was definitely going back home to Montana. Tammy knew that Brynn would be thrilled. If Amy didn't want to move with them Tammy would ask Robert to make arrangements for Amy to stay in LA.

"Hi, I'm home," Tammy called, walking into the house.

She was greeted by three excited bassets, Jude, and Brynn.

"Hello, Aunt Tammy," Brynn said, running up to her and throwing her arms around Tammy.

Brynn would do this every time Tammy returned home. It was like she was afraid Tammy wasn't coming back, something Tammy could completely understand after the child's loss.

"Hey, honey, how was your day?" Tammy asked Brynn, giving her a big hug and a kiss on the head.

"Jude and I collected a lot of shells." Brynn smiled up at her.

"I hope you're going to show them to me?" Tammy put her arm around Brynn's shoulder as she walked into the living room with the three bassets running around their feet excitedly.

"Of course," Brynn promised. "Jude was also teaching me some defense moves."

"Oh, that's cool." Tammy looked at Jude who stood professionally to one side watching them and mouthed a thank you. Jude gave a smile and nodded. "There's something I want to discuss with you."

"Oh?" Brynn's head shot up, and anxious eyes met Tammy's.

"How do you feel about going back home to Montana?" Tammy asked her and was startled by the look of shock that paled on Brynn's face.

"You don't want me to live here with you anymore?" Brynn's voice was rough with emotion and her eyes misted over.

"Oh, no, honey it's not that," Tammy pulled Brynn into her arms and could feel her shaking. "I'm sorry. I'm still getting used to this. What I should've said is 'how do you feel about us moving back to Montana'?"

Tammy felt her niece's little shoulders sag with relief, and she put her small arms around Tammy's waist.

"I want to be where you are, Aunt Tammy," Brynn said softly, resting her head on Tammy's chest. "I don't want you to leave me alone. I'm happy to stay here with you."

"That's so sweet." Tammy's heart broke for her niece. "But my job is to make sure you're safe and happy."

Tammy pulled Brynn a little closer and when she looked over

to where Jude had been, she noticed he'd quietly slipped away, leaving them to have their family moment.

"Do you want to go home to Montana?" Brynn asked Tammy.

"To be honest, I really do." Tammy sighed and put her head on Brynn's. "I've wanted to go home for a while now."

"I do too," Brynn admitted. "I miss my horse, the ranch, my friends, and Constance."

"I do too honey." Tammy stroked Brynn's soft hair. "Do you think April, Craven, and Derby are going to like Montana?"

Brynn sat back and looked at Tammy. Excitement flashed in the child's eyes.

"I think they're going to love it," Brynn said. "I know just where we can put their beds."

"Oh?" Tammy smiled. "Where?"

"In my room." Brynn grinned.

Hearing their names, the bassets jumped up on the sofa, squashing Tammy, and Brynn as they laughed at the crazy dogs.

"Now all I need to do is talk to Amy and Jude," Tammy said to Brynn, who now had two bassets fighting over her tiny lap.

"I'm sure Aunt Amy will come with us too." Brynn patiently patted the two dogs. "She asked me about Montana yesterday."

"Oh?" Tammy looked at Brynn questioningly. "Why did she do that?"

"She asked me if I wanted to go back there." Brynn laughed as Derby knocked her hand when she stopped patting him. "She told me that she wouldn't mind going there for a while."

Tammy nodded and stared at Brynn for a few minutes. "Where is Amy?" She looked around.

"She had another headache and went to lie down," Brynn told Tammy.

"I'll go check on her," Tammy said, standing up. "Are you okay here?"

"I'm fine," Brynn assured Tammy, but Tammy noticed she looked around for Jude, who mysteriously appeared on cue.

"Jude, how would you feel about following us to Montana?"

Tammy knew that Brynn had grown fond of Jude. She also seemed to be a lot less anxious and scared when he was around.

"I would need to clear it with the agency, and you'd have to discuss it with them," Jude told her. "But I wouldn't mind moving to Montana." He grinned.

"Your family won't mind the move?" Tammy asked, fishing about his marital status. She suddenly realized she hadn't even asked him about that.

"It's just me," Jude assured her. "I'll leave you to make the call to the agency?"

"I'll do that," Tammy promised. "I have to go check on and speak to Amy."

Jude nodded and walked over to Brynn, "Hey, kid, I'm starving. Why don't we go make a snack? I'm sure these three would also like a snack."

"I'm hungry too," Brynn told Jude, gently moving the dogs so she could stand up and take the large hand he'd held out to her. "Will you make that super-duper delicious sandwich of yours?"

"Yup," Jude nodded, walking into the kitchen, holding Brynn's hand, and followed by three eager bassets.

Tammy smiled. She'd gotten really lucky with Jude. The dogs, Amy, and Brynn trusted him. But the main thing is that they all felt safe with him around. Right now, they all needed some sense of security. Tammy walked to Amy's room and softly knocked on the door.

"Amy?" Tammy called through the door. "Can I come in?"

"Sure," Amy said. Tammy could hear her voice was muffled.

Tammy walked into the dark room and found Amy lying on the bed with an ice pack on her head.

"You need to take those pills the doctor gave you, Amy," Tammy told her. "You can't go on like this."

"I don't want to take any pills," Amy said. "Look what happened the last time when I hurt my shoulder doing a stunt for a movie. Martin had me committed for abusing painkillers."

"Amy..." Tammy sat on the edge of the bed. "You were in

pain. You had to have an operation on that shoulder and then you got that bone marrow infection in it."

"Osteomyelitis," Amy told her. "Still, I shouldn't have become so dependent on those painkillers." She went silent for a few minutes before grabbing Tammy's hand for support.

"Tammy, I was so dependent on them that I don't even remember buying them." Amy's voice wobbled with disgust and self-loathing. "Martin was right to do what he did now that I think about it."

"Let's not dwell on that right now," Tammy told her, gently taking back her hand so she could feel the ice pack. "Why don't I make you some peppermint tea and give you a less addictive migraine cocktail I take when I get one."

"I'll try anything right now," Amy said.

Tammy could see her eyes were glassy with the pain.

"I'll bring you a new ice pack as well." Tammy fluffed up Amy's pillow. "Are you feeling nausea this time?"

"No," Amy tried to shake her head and immediately regretted it. "My nose didn't bleed this time either."

"That's good." Tammy smiled down at her. "I'll be right back with the tea and pills."

"Okay." Amy closed her eyes again.

Tammy walked out of the room. She stopped at the door glancing worriedly at Amy. Something about the time Martin had Amy committed didn't sit well with Tammy. She knew Amy, and the woman only ever drank no more than half a glass of wine. Amy never touched hard spirits and would rather drink peppermint tea for a headache than take pills. She always tried alternative medication rather than conventional medication. Amy was obsessed with not using anything like painkillers. It didn't make sense to Tammy that she would become addicted or reliant on them. And how did a person not remember buying pain pills? Also, these days you could just keep fulfilling painkiller prescriptions.

Something was very wrong with that entire Amy story. Tammy wondered if Jude was up for doing some investigative work for her. Tammy walked through to the kitchen where she found Jude, Brynn, and the bassets sitting on a picnic blanket on the floor, eating.

"The wind has picked up outside so we're having a picnic in here," Jude told her.

"We didn't want to make a mess on the living room carpet," Brynn said.

Each of the bassets gave a bark to have their say in the conversation as if they understood what was being said. Tammy's heart started to melt as she smiled down at them. It was so nice to be part of a family again!

Chapter Five
HOME TO DOUBLE A RANCH

CURRENT DAY

"Wow!" Brynn and Amy said as they admired the brand-new Lexus waiting for them at the Billings, Montana, airport.

"I thought we'd need an SUV for the ranch," Tammy told them with a grin.

"So instead of a normal pickup, you went for the top-of-the-line model?" Amy laughed. "Not that I'm complaining." She hopped into the front passenger seat.

"Awesome!" Brynn sang, sitting in the luxurious seat behind Amy. She immediately started exploring the compartments and gadgets.

"I took one for a test drive in LA, and I fell in love with it." Tammy climbed into the driver's seat and snapped on her seatbelt. "Are you two ladies ready to go home?"

"Yes!" Both Amy and Brynn shouted enthusiastically.

"Are the dogs going to be okay in the back?" Brynn asked.

"They're still a bit dopey from the trip," Tammy told her, pulling out of the parking place. "We'll need to stop in a while to let them out once they've fully recovered."

"I have their leashes," Brynn said.

"Great." Tammy drove them out of the airport and headed for the highway to take them to Lewistown. "We have a good two-hour drive ahead of us, so I hope you're all comfy?"

"Who wouldn't be, in this car?" Amy fidgeted with the front gadgets.

"I have all the snacks back here if anyone gets hungry," Brynn called from the back. "I'm also putting on my headphones now and looking for something to watch."

"You do that, honey," Tammy said, glancing at Brynn in the mirror to ensure she had her seatbelt on. The car would tell her if she didn't, but Tammy remembered her brother liked to snap it in behind him. Brian hated seatbelts, which used to drive his wife and Tammy crazy with worry for him when he drove. Not to mention the hefty fine he'd get if he got stopped by a patrol car. "Just not too loud, though, I don't want you hurting your ears."

"Tammy, this car is amazing." Amy was fiddling with the center console. "I need to get my license back. I miss driving."

"Let's put that on ice for now." Tammy glanced at Amy, who was now watching the countryside go by. "You need to remember how to ride a horse because that's the transport you're going to be using when we get to the ranch."

"I'm looking forward to riding again." Amy drew her attention away from the window to look at Tammy. "Brynn has told me all about her horses on the farm. I can't wait to see them."

"Ranch," Tammy corrected her.

"I thought all ranches were farms?" Amy said. "The only thing that differs is that a ranch is usually a lot bigger, and livestock is its main focus, while a farm's main focus is its land cultivation."

"You've been Googling, haven't you?" Tammy laughed. "But you can get some pretty massive farms."

"So, your ranch only does cattle?" Amy asked.

"Yes, and we breed quarter horses," Tammy told her. "We never used to sell the horses we bred. My parents bred the horses to use on the ranch, but my brother turned that around. He joined forces with a neighboring ranch's breeding program, Cupids Bow Ranch."

"That's Cat Sparrow's ranch, right?" Amy looked out of the window again. "I can't believe all the wide-open space."

"Yes, Cupids Bow belongs to the Sparrow family, and it is where Cat grew up." Tammy glanced out of her window at the rolling prairies running alongside them. "Yes, there is tons of wild open space out here."

Tammy smiled. With every mile closer she got to Double A she began to feel more peaceful. Tammy opened her window so she could let in the country air and took a deep breath. It was so good to be able to breathe again. Excitement made her stomach clench as she thought about sitting on her back porch with a cup of cocoa later that evening. She could gaze up at the dark sky, lit by a myriad of sparkling silver stars and enjoy the quiet.

"When is Jude joining us?" Brynn suddenly asked from the back seat.

"Jude will be here in a few days," Tammy looked at Brynn in the mirror. "He needed to finalize his affairs."

"Okay." Brynn nodded and put her headphones back on. "That's good."

"Brynn adores Jude," Amy said. "I think she feels safe with him by her side or watching out for all of us."

"I know." Tammy smiled at Amy. "The accident on the ski slopes has her so rattled. I'm glad you're both here with her. It gives her a sense of family."

"I think all of us being together gives us all a sense of family," Amy voiced Tammy's thoughts and feelings. "We've only got each other now."

"That's why I was so happy that you wanted to move to Montana with us," Tammy said honestly. "I also think it's just what you need right now."

"I know," Amy agreed. "I'm glad that you suggested it because I was going to."

"Brynn told me." Tammy noticed Derby's head pop up on the back seat. "I think our other passengers have woken up."

"Are you going to pull over?" Amy asked.

"I have to," Tammy said and noticed the look of fear that darkened Amy's eyes. "You and Brynn can stay in the car if you like."

"No," Amy shook her head. "I'll help with one of the bassets."

"If you're sure." Tammy found a safe place to pull over where she stopped the car.

"I'll also help with the bassets," Brynn said, looking over at the back. "Hello, you three. How are you feeling?"

Tammy got out of the car and walked around the back to open the door. She was greeted by three dogs who were still a little disoriented. Tammy hooked their leads on. Amy took Derby, Brynn took Craven, and Tammy took April. They let the dogs have a walk down by the side of a fenced-off field that was a little way back from the road.

"It is so peaceful out here," Amy sighed.

"I've missed this quiet." Tammy leaned down and patted April's head. "Are either of you hungry?"

"I could eat." Amy looked at her.

"I'm starving!" Brynn came to stand next to them while the three bassets sniffed around. "Do you know that bassets have two-hundred and twenty-million smell receptors? Their long ears also sweep smells up to their incredibly sharp noses."

"No," Tammy admitted. "I did not know that."

"That is amazing!" Amy looked at Brynn, impressed.

"I've been researching them in the car on that amazing system it has." Brynn grinned. "Their legs are also that short to keep their noses in perfect proportion to the ground for smelling. That's why they are so perfect at following scents."

"You have been doing your research." Amy laughed. "I do know that they originated in France and that the word basset comes from the French word 'bas,' which means 'close to the ground'."

"I was just about to say that!" Tammy's eyes narrowed at Amy. "You stole my bit of knowledge."

"You were too slow." Amy grinned.

"They are amazing little fur people, Aunt Tammy." Brynn knelt and hugged Craven. She was soon bombarded by the other two, who wanted their love as well. Brynn was pushed over by and giggled as the bassets gave her doggie kisses.

"Okay, you lot." Tammy laughed. "Time to get back on the road."

"Shouldn't we let the dogs have a few more minutes?" Amy looked at them worriedly. "They drank a heck of a lot of water."

"They'll let us know if they need to stop again," Tammy assured Amy, walking the dogs back to the car.

She opened the back. The dogs obediently jumped in while Brynn and Amy climbed into the car. As Tammy made her way around to the driver's side, she stopped as she noticed a parked car facing their way a few miles down the road on the opposite side. She frowned. Tammy was sure she'd seen a similar car pull out of the airport in Billings. Tammy shook it off. She was just being paranoid. The person was obviously lost as they had what looked like a map open in front of them. Still, a cold shiver ran up her spine and she gave a shudder while climbing into the driver's seat of her brand-new SUV. As she pulled off and drove past the car, Tammy memorized the license plate.

A few hours later, they had just bypassed Lewistown and turned off towards Double A Ranch when two police cars and an ambulance flew past them.

"Good grief, I wonder what's happening?" Tammy said and as she said that the same cold feeling, she'd had the night of the avalanche crept up her spine.

"Uh... Tammy," Amy said, looking at her wide-eyed. "Why have you sped up?"

"I have a bad feeling," was all Tammy would say as she tried her best to keep up with the emergency vehicles without being pulled over by another cop car.

"Aunt Tammy," Brynn sounded distressed. "Are those emergency vehicles headed towards the Double A?"

"I'm not sure, honey," Tammy didn't quite know how to answer, so she decided to go with the truth.

"Well, then, can't this fancy contraption go any faster?" Amy asked, suddenly sounding panicked.

Tammy glanced over to find Amy's face had paled, "Are you okay?"

"I..." Amy looked at Tammy with fear and panic glowing in her eyes. "I'm sorry, I just had these terrible flashbacks of a sea of white hurtling down on us," she said softly so Brynn couldn't hear.

"It's okay." Tammy reached over and gave Amy's hand an encouraging squeeze. "Do the exercises your doctor gave you."

Amy nodded, put her head back against that headrest, and did her breathing techniques.

The closer they got to Double A, the more Tammy's heartbeat accelerated, no longer from excitement but from the dread of finding the emergency vehicles parked in her yard. The minute she turned into the drive she knew her fears were true. As she looked into her mirror, her brow furrowed into a deep frown as she saw the car that was parked across from them drive past.

What is going on? Tammy suppressed a shudder and drove slowly up the drive then around the back of the house where they usually parked. When they turned the corner, her blood froze in her veins upon seeing the emergency vehicles and a lot of cars.

"What on earth is going on?" Tammy said before looking at Amy and Brynn. "Please, both of you stay here until I know what's happened."

She looked at Brynn, who nodded, and Amy did the same, "Keep an eye on the dogs."

Tammy took off her seatbelt and climbed out of her car. The first thing she noticed was all the people who were standing around Constance turned to watch her walk towards them. Tammy refused to let their curious eyes phase her or make her feel intimidated. That may have been young or teenage Tammy, but she was no longer that shy girl. She was now a confident woman, and they were all trespassing on her property. If anything, it should be Tammy eyeing them all out questioningly before cross-examining them all.

Just before Tammy neared the group of people, she heard Brynn shout from behind her.

"Constance!" Brynn ran towards the Andersons' long-time housekeeper.

"Oh, my pumpkin," Constance's eyes misted over, and a few big teardrops rolled down her rosy cheeks. "I've missed you so much, my little angel." She kissed Brynn's shiny golden head before giving her a big squeeze.

"What on earth is going on here?" Tammy walked up to where the group was standing. She recognized her neighbors Maria, Cat, and Chelsea. They were standing with a man who looked too young to be wearing the Police Captain's badge.

"As I live and breathe," Constance kept an arm around Brynn's small shoulders and watched happily as Tammy walked over to greet her. "Is that you, Tammy Anderson?" Her voice wobbled with emotion.

"Hello, Connie." Tammy pulled her oversized designer sunglasses off to lean forward to accept Constance's greeting and embrace. "It's been too long." She looked at the three women standing next to Constance, gaping at her. "It's rude to stare, you know." She smiled teasingly at them. "Didn't I try and tell at least two of you that?" She pointed at Cat and Chelsea.

"Tammy!" Maria Parker looked at her in astonishment. "You haven't changed a bit."

"Hello, Maria," Tammy greeted her with a hug. "It's good to see you." She stopped talking and looked at the police captain before glancing at the emergency vehicles. "What is going on?" She looked back at Chelsea, Maria, and Cat.

"Miss Anderson?" The young police captain stammered. "Uh... mam, where have you been all day?"

Tammy's brows shot up as she looked at the man in confusion, watching as his cheeks turned a bright shade of red when her attention was drawn to him. *Is he questioning me about something?*

Maria took pity on him, "Tammy, I think what the police captain is trying to say is, when did you get into town?" Maria gave the young police captain a pitying look and shook her head.

"We've only just arrived," Tammy said, a little indignant. *The man is questioning me like I'm a suspect.* He looked familiar to Tammy. "Why? And why have I still not been told what the heck is going on, on *my* property?"

Tammy didn't mean to use what Uncle Robert and Brenda called her 'corporate' voice, a voice and attitude she'd mastered early on in her career. It's what kept arrogant stars in place and made them realize although they were her clients, they needed her. She was there to clean up a mess or make them look good. She didn't need anyone to do the same for her. Tammy's posture mimicked her voice to show who was in control and her eyes narrowed as she looked at the police captain.

"There was an explosion in the mountains earlier," Maria once again stepped in for the clumsy police captain, who was still gaping at Tammy like a goldfish. "Most of the ranches and their hands went to fight the fire its explosion caused. We realized too late it was a diversion." She pointed at Tammy's stables, her eyes darkening in anger.

"You mean the thugs that have been plaguing the land have now cleaned both my stables and livestock out?" Tammy stared wide-eyed at Maria. Shock tingled through her body. That was not what Tammy needed to hear right now. "And this all happened not even more than a couple of hours ago?"

Maria nodded in confirmation. "And a young girl, Maggie, has been taken by Pete."

"Pete?" Tammy's perfect brow creased into a frown. She

looked at Constance. "*Our* Pete that's been here since before my granddad retired?"

"I'm afraid so, honey," Constance said, something flashing in her eyes, making Tammy frown. "If you don't mind, I'm going to take young Brynn here away from all this commotion. I really don't think she should be exposed to it all."

"Yes, please." Tammy gave Constance a thankful nod and smiled at a very pale Brynn.

Oh no, she's terrified again! Tammy made a mental note to find out when exactly Jude would arrive. Brynn settled when he was around. Tammy looked around at the car, noticing Amy was half in and half out, fidgeting with something. "Amy!" She yelled. "What the devil are you doing in there?"

"Sorry, I was trying to find my ring that slipped down between the seats," Amy grumbled. "I guess I'll have to come back with a flashlight."

She jumped out of the car, and Tammy was too distracted to notice that the police officer was no longer the only one gaping like a goldfish.

"Please let the dogs out of the back," Tammy called. "I'm sure they are very eager to get out by now."

"Sure," Amy called, walking around the car to open the back, and let the three eager bassets out of the car.

The three dogs didn't even prance around or sniff the air. They each quickly did a little business, then dashed into the house where they knew Brynn had gone.

Traitors! Tammy smiled to herself, knowing that Constance was going to have a fit when those three barreled into the house.

"Oh, hi," Amy gave a big smile and a wave as she walked closer to where Tammy was standing. "Looks like we arrived just in time for all the action."

"Why don't you go inside," Tammy suggested, seeing what a stir Amy, America's sweetheart and one of the top-grossing actresses of all time, was creating. "You can help Constance with Brynn.

"But..." Amy, who was at least a head and a half shorter than Tammy, craned her neck to look up at her. "I want to know what's going on here."

"I'll fill you in later," Tammy's voice brooked no argument.

"It was nice almost meeting you all," Amy said, turning to walk off. Then, she stopped. Turning back, she gave everyone next to Tammy a beaming smile. Tammy knew that look well–it was the one she used for her adoring fans. "I'm Amy, by the way."

"I'm Maria, this is Cat, and that is Chelsea." Maria introduced the three of them. "This is our new police captain. Parker Watson."

"Watson?" Tammy's head shot around towards the man, her eyes once again narrowing as she looked at him. "Do you have kin in Lewistown?"

"Yes, mam," Parker looked cautiously at Tammy, and she could've sworn he leaned slightly away from her like she was about to slap him.

Tammy's whole body stiffened, and her jaw clenched. It took everything she had to stop her fists from curling into tight, angry fists at her sides and keep her erratic heart under control.

"Are you related to Sam Watson?" Tammy said through gritted teeth feeling her eyes instantly narrow a little more at the mention of the Watson name.

"Yes, mam, he was my granddad." This time, Parker took a step back.

Tammy saw his Adam's apple bob nervously in his throat as he stared at Tammy with a look of fear in his eyes. Tammy was used to that look. It was the one spoiled entitled celebrities or corporate heads gave her when they'd pushed her too far and suddenly realized their futures were actually in her hands. Tammy knew the sins of one or a few family members weren't the sins of the entire family. But that family had a special place in Tammy's memories and heart. Filed under 'repulsive, hateful, snakes — avoid at all costs.'

"Who's your father?" Tammy's voice dropped only slightly but held a dangerous edge to it.

"Arnold Green," Parker told her, swallowing nervously, his eyes widening a little more. "I kept my mother's name as her and my father never married. He split up with her before I was born." He spilled out all his personal information like he'd been interrogated by the CIA, staring warily at Tammy.

Tammy turned her attention away from Parker, trying not to let his story pull at her heartstrings. She knew exactly who his mother was. Tammy pushed away the guilt that was trying to break through her icy reserve that came out whenever she heard the name Watson. She turned her attention back to her three neighbors standing staring at her curiously.

"You said a girl had been kidnapped from here today?" Tammy asked Maria.

"Yes, her name is Maggie," Maria told Tammy.

"Who is Maggie?" Tammy asked, confused. *Was she one of the ranch hands' daughters? Does Constance have a granddaughter I don't know about?* Her brows furrowed.

"My daughter!" A deep voice resonated from just behind her.

Tammy's shoulders instantly stiffened. This time she couldn't stop her hands from clenching into fists at her side. A fit of strong red-hot anger shot up from her belly and hit her heart, making it ring with a myriad of emotions making it pound in her chest. Tammy noticed all heads turned towards the man standing behind her. She didn't need to turn around to know he was a tall, broad-shouldered cowboy, with intense green eyes splashed with gold. His handsome face was framed by dark slightly wavy hair with a bonus of a dimpled killer smile that had slain more women than Tammy could probably count.

He was also the one man Tammy had hoped would be the last she'd run into back home in Montana. She knew he was living back here, and their meeting would be inevitable, but Tammy didn't want to, nor did she have the time to ponder on that when she'd left LA. To her utter dismay and without her wanting to know, Brian had kept her updated. He'd start by telling her about their ranch neighbors and then move to his friends in Lewistown where he'd slot in the information.

It took her a few seconds to get herself under control from the shock of hearing his deep voice, which had vibrated through her system like an echo. Only this time, she didn't let her soul answer.

Chapter Six
THE WRONG DAY FOR A HOMECOMING

She was no longer an eighteen-year-old that could be used or trod on. Tammy sifted through the information in her brain and landed on the fact that Maggie was Greg's daughter. *What was Maggie doing on my ranch?* She made herself focus on that as well as, *What the heck is Greg Watson doing on my ranch?* Tammy felt a little more in control now. He was on her property, her ground! She slowly turned around and pulled the icy barrier back up around her thudding heart, stilling it as she dropped a curtain of indifference over her feelings. It was a trick she'd learned to do in the world she'd stepped into in LA, to protect herself from the sharks that would eat her alive at the first whiff of blood.

"Hi, Greg," Parker stepped forward, nearly knocking Tammy over as he eagerly went to greet his uncle. "I'm so sorry about Maggie. I promise I'm making it the station's top priority to find her. We already have a BOLO out on Pete Ferguson."

"Tammy?" Another deep voice caught her attention, keeping her from looking at Greg. She knew she was deliberately avoiding him. Tammy could feel that was making him even more irritated than the sight of her must've done. Greg hated being ignored. "What were you thinking, rushing out here on your own when you knew it was potentially dangerous?"

Tammy took a little bit of perverted pleasure knowing Greg's eyes were now boring into her. She could feel them on her just like she'd always been able to do. Only back then she'd mistaken his intense looks for something else. This time Tammy knew without a shadow of a doubt what look she was going to find in Greg Watson's eyes when finally decided to acknowledge his presence.

"She wasn't alone," Cat told him. "Chelsea and I were with her."

"And that makes it all better?" Zac hissed, coming up behind West and inserting himself between Cat and Chelsea. "You nearly gave us all heart failure – not to mention you made us punish our horses, pushing them so hard to get here at the speed of light."

"Where's Brett?" Maria looked at Zac.

Tammy noticed that Maria's attention seemed to be caught by something behind Zac. Before she could follow Maria's gaze, West answered Maria's question, keeping her focus on West.

"He's okay," West assured her. "We told him to stay behind as he's one of the few that know how to operate that fire hose he has."

"I'd better call him," Maria said, stepping away from the group.

Tammy watched Maria stride away with her phone in her hand, but she had a feeling Maria had seen something. As her eyes took the path Maria was taking, they collided with the icy ones of Greg Watson's. Her jaw once again clenched, and her eyes narrowed to match his as their gazes locked in a silent war. Tammy didn't know how long they stood glaring at each other waiting for the first one to greet the other when their staring match was interrupted by Maria. Saving them both from having to be the first one to say hello.

"Greg," Maria called, stepping up to him. "I think I found Maggie's phone in the bush."

"You did?" Greg broke eye contact as soon as he'd heard mention of his daughter.

But before they did, Tammy had seen the intense look of love and fear that had flowed into them. Tammy felt as if she'd been shot in the heart with a flood of the most powerful emotions she'd ever felt by that look. She knew the look wasn't meant for her, but she'd still felt its power. Greg Watson did have a heart after all, but the only one with access to it was his daughter.

"Does she have an Apple Watch by chance?" Maria asked him.

"Yes," Greg scratched his forehead beneath his hat. "She bothered me for months to get that blasted thing. She was supposed to put some tracking app on my phone."

Tammy watched the emotions flitter through Greg's eyes and that his hand shook ever so slightly when touched his hat. It was a look she'd never seen on him in all the time she'd known him. He looked vulnerable, and Tammy felt the walls of her icy resolve start to get hairline cracks in them.

Oh no you don't, Tammy Anderson! Tammy admonished herself. *Greg Watson may seem human where his daughter is concerned, but, to everyone else, he's still The Terminator*, she reminded herself. Still, a tiny traitorous part of her admired his obvious love and devotion to his young daughter. Another twinge of emotion she refused to acknowledge tried to tug at her. The same emotion she'd lived with as a young girl and through her teenage life. Tammy took a deep mental breath and went to her place of strength to shake off those silly, childish insecurities that she locked away so long ago. She would not let one meeting with Greg Watson rip through her like that!

"Well, she loaded that app on her phone and dropped it into the bush so we could find her with that blasted watch." Maria showed him.

Maria's voice brought Tammy out of her deep thoughts, making her concentrate on what was going on around her and bringing her back to the problem at hand.

"Can you zoom in on that location?" Parker asked Maria, hanging over Maria's shoulder to get a look at the phone.

"Yes," Maria looked over her shoulder at him, nodding. She zoomed in. "Bingo!" She breathed. "Let's go get her."

Maria spun on her heel to head towards a pickup truck when West stopped her by putting his hand on her shoulder. Tammy watched the interaction between the two and instinctively knew something was going on between them. It seemed like it was still new by the way they interacted with each, but there was definitely something budding.

"Wait up," West growled. "There is no way I can let you go traipsing off into a potentially dangerous situation. I promised your brother I'd keep an eye on you."

"Well, that's just too bad," Maria told him, giving him a look that Tammy had always admired Maria for. It was a look that told the person it was aimed at that there was nothing short of knocking her out and dragging her away that would change her mind. "Because I'm going. Besides, no one else here seems to know how to work this app." She told him smugly. "So, either you come with, or you stay behind."

"I'll drive," Greg sauntered past them, holding his hand out to Maria presumably for the keys to the pickup she was standing next to. "You can't navigate and drive."

"Sure," Maria handed him the keys.

"Wait, we're coming too," Cat and Chelsea ran towards Maria's truck.

"You're going to have to go in another car," Tammy informed them, stepping around the two women. "That's my land, so I need to be there."

"Fine, we'll take my truck," Chelsea offered to hand Zac the keys. "You can drive."

"I'll follow in the squad car and get back up to meet us at the location," Parker told them.

Three vehicles and the ambulance pulled off to head towards the location Maggie's watch was pinging from. Maria was seated next to Greg in the front of the vehicle navigating the way. While Tammy and West were at the back.

West gave Tammy a big smile, and her hand a hidden gentle squeeze, saying softly for her ears only, "How are you?"

"Bewildered!" Tammy answered equally quietly, giving his hand a little squeeze back in a silent thanks for his support.

Out of all her brothers' friends, West was always the one she could count on to be on her

side. But throughout their entire professional lives, Tammy and West had kept their friendship a secret. As two high-profile executives, Tammy didn't want the world to think the only reason she got to where she was now had been because of who her family and friends were. She'd wanted credit for the hours she'd slogged away, and all the extra effort she'd had to put in to climb to where she was. Tammy had managed to keep her reputation squeaky clean until the Martin scandal.

Given her job, it was imperative. Even the Martin scandal had not tarnished her reputation. Her PR firm had seen to that. But it had put quite a bad dent into Martin's, and unfortunately, it had also unlatched the closet all his skeletons were shoved in. There was nothing Tammy could do to help him as her firm had told her to step out of his mess. She'd worked too hard and was finally near the finish line to let Martin drag her down with him. Tammy liked to put on a hard shell, but it had still eaten her alive inside, knowing that she was the final hole in Martin's fast sinking ship that had finally made him go down. The only way Tammy was able to stop herself from defying her firm and helping him was by picturing the day she'd found in their spa with Ursula. Even now, after all these years it still stung like someone pouring salt into a festering wound.

Tammy's attention snapped back to the present as they turned onto the dirt road that led to one of the cabins. She knew they were used for cattle drives on her ranch. She craned her neck to look out the small window as she heard the sound of a helicopter circling up ahead.

Greg called Parker and told him to tell the helicopter to pull back as they didn't want to spook the men. Greg also suggested that only his vehicle goes up to the main house and the rest of them hold back until Maria calls them to descend upon the property. Greg didn't want anyone getting harmed and thought it best if only one vehicle rode up there. He tried to convince Maria, West, and Tammy to get into one of the other vehicles and let him go in alone, but the three of them refused. Greg had no option but to drive them to the cabin with him.

"Are those my cattle and horses?" Tammy hissed, noticing the tags on the cattle as they drove near the cabin. On the other side of the drive were a lot of horses. She was sure some also belonged to her.

"Not all of them," Greg said, not taking his eyes off the cabin. "I think some of them must also be from the other ranches around here that have lost livestock lately."

"They've been holding stolen animals on my ranch?" Tammy's eyes widened in dismay and her eyes met the compassionate ones of Maria's, who turned to look her way.

"Don't worry, I think this time we got lucky, and at least some of the ranches will recover their animals," Maria told her.

"I can't believe that I picked today of all days to arrive back home," Tammy said incredulously.

"You do tend to have a knack for walking in at the wrong moment," Greg's voice was filled with anger and barbed sarcasm as his icy eyes looked at Tammy in the mirror.

Tammy felt the red-hot anger that had simmered down to a slow burn start to quickly bubble inside of her once again. But she refused to let Greg see that he could rile her like that, so Tammy chose to ignore his remark, glancing at him with cool indifference instead. As she glanced away, she caught the look West shot the back of Greg's head, and once again, Tammy reached over to give West's hand a squeeze letting him know to ignore it. West looked at her apologetically as if he was atoning for Greg's sins. Tammy gave an inward sigh. West had always been so level-headed and the diplomat out of her brother's group of friends.

"They know we're here," Greg said. Drawing Tammy's attention to the cottage. His eyes never left the house. "Maggie's in there."

"According to her phone, she is," Maria concluded. "Why are you stopping here?" She looked at him. "Let's go in there. We have the police behind us."

"No," Greg said, switching off the engine and releasing his seatbelt. "I need to go in there alone."

"What are you doing?" Maria asked, giving him a sideways look as if he was out of his mind. "You can't go out there on your own."

If only Maria knew just how gung-ho and irresponsible a riled-up angry Greg Watson could be, she'd be shocked. He was a master of fooling the world around him that he was some sort of 'good guy' hero. But he was a fraud that cared for no one but himself and got what he wanted no matter who he had to go through.

"They have my daughter," Greg said. "They are not going to harm me. If they took Maggie, it's for a reason that concerns me. That means they need me alive to cooperate."

"Yes, but now you're barricading their only exit," Tammy pointed out, knowing that the only other way out of that cabin was to one side as they backdropped into a steep cliff. "There is a steep cliff at the back of the cottage. The only way out is to the East on horseback or through the drive we are parked in."

"Are you concerned about me?" Greg asked her mockingly, once again catching her eyes in the mirror.

"No," Tammy said as emotionlessly as she could. "I am concerned about the thieves making a getaway on one of my horses or your innocent daughter getting harmed because she has an idiot for a father."

She raised an eyebrow, holding his stare in the mirror.

"Do you have a better idea, Miss Fixer?" Greg's eyes narrowed as he glared at Tammy.

"Not yet," Tammy admitted, she did but she doubted the macho fool would let her even voice it let alone carry out her plan. "But I don't think you getting out to try to be a hero is the answer."

"I don't have time for you to put a full-blown strategy presentation together so you can fix the situation." Greg's voice was filled with contempt and was bubbling with anger. He looked at Maria. "Keep an eye on Maggie's position." He looked at West in the mirror. "I need you to call Zac and tell him I need him to try to sneak around the back to assess the situation."

"Sure." West took out his phone to call Zac. Tammy saw West frown when she heard Chelsea answer the phone. "Chelsea, where is Zac?"

"He's disappeared into the tree line," Chelsea's voice was a little loud, giving away the panic in it. "I tried to stop him."

"I think Zac has already gone to assess the situation," West told Greg, who nodded as he slid out of the pickup, closing the door behind him.

Tammy noted that Maria hardly pulled her eyes off Maggie's phone. Tammy was about to tell them about her idea on how to deal with the situation when all their attention was drawn to the cabin.

"Don't take another step," a voice boomed from somewhere to the left of the house.

All the window blinds had been drawn. It took a minute for Tammy to locate the window from which the unmistakable glint of a rifle barrel could be seen sticking through.

"I'm not here for any trouble," Greg shouted to them. "All I want is my daughter."

Tammy watched, her breath caught in her throat and her heart nearly stopping in her chest when Greg put his hands in the air and took a cautionary step in front of the vehicle. As soon as Greg had taken that step a shot cracked the air like a thunderbolt splitting the sky. Tammy, Maria, and even West jumped but only Tammy and Maria ducked down. Tammy's head turned to eye West frantically willing him to duck down as her heart pounded in fear.

"Tell your friends in the vehicle to back up and leave," the man called out. "We'll not negotiate with ya until you're alone, though we're happy you're unarmed."

Is that Samuel Yates? Tammy suddenly realized who the man behind the voice might be. She looked at West, pulled out her phone, and messaged him, not wanting to draw Maria's attention.

> *Message Zac that the man with the gun on Greg is Samuel Yates. One of Zac's ranch hands. He's Pete's half-brother.*

West got the message and looked up at Tammy in surprise, nodded, and started to message Zac. Tammy and Maria both sat back up to see what was going on outside the vehicle.

"No," Greg disagreed, shaking his head. "My friends stay." *Typical Greg*, Tammy thought having to have everything on his terms. "I also warn you that if you harm one hair on my daughter's head, you'll be sorry."

Tammy saw Maria's head turn to the right, and Tammy saw a shadowy figure slip into the line of trees that ran to the one side of the cabin. Her father had always threatened to have them cut down because they concealed a dangerous drop just a few meters into the thicket of them.

"There's someone out there who has just moved into the woods after Zac," Maria said. "We need to warn him."

"Zac can take care of himself," West reminded her. Tammy noted how his voice took on a soft quality when he spoke to Maria, and she smiled to herself. It would be nice to see two such special people together. They both deserved so much more than what their exes had done to them. "He's been trained for this type of operation. I'm sure he already knows someone is following him."

"I'm sure I've seen the man who slipped into the woods before," Maria said, squinting into the tree line. "Even though I only got a glimpse of him, there was something in the way that he moved."

Before Tammy could ask questions, Greg once again grabbed their attention. Tammy once again found her breath catching in her throat, thinking the arrogant man was going to get himself killed.

"I'm not looking for trouble," Greg tried to reassure whoever was pointing a rifle at them. "I just want my daughter back, so why don't you tell me what it is you want?"

"Grayson," the man said.

Tammy's eyes narrowed at the mention of that name. They surely couldn't be talking about... She gave her head a shake. No, there was no way. Why on earth would they want Grayson? It didn't make any sense to her. Tammy would understand if they wanted Greg, but not Grayson. Maria turned to look back at Tammy and West with confusion in her big eyes and her brows were tightly drawn together.

"Who's Grayson?" She turned and looked questioningly at Tammy. "Do you know a Grayson?"

Tammy was about to answer Maria when she caught the warning look West shot her, making her go against her better judgment and lie to one of her only friends she had in Montana.

"No," Tammy said, shaking her head as the lie tumbled uncomfortably from her lips, making her automatically switch into what Tammy called 'liar's mode'. That was overcompensating for the lie by embellishing it, but she couldn't help it. She felt like a ladybug that had just been caught in a big ugly spider's web as she blurted, "I've only ever heard of one Grayson, but I've never met or seen him. I doubt very much he's even been to Montana."

"Are you talking about Grayson Wyatt?" West asked her, trying to help her out as he picked up on her distress. "The reclusive best-selling author?"

"Yes," Tammy smiled gratefully at West, trying not to let Maria see her unease and hoping she couldn't hear hard her heart was pounding against her ribs. But once the lie had started, she tried to smooth it over with some truth, "I worked on some PR for him. But I was not allowed to meet him in person. We took a conference call over the internet, but no cameras were allowed."

Her eyes traveled to West, silently asking him to jump in again as Tammy felt her lies starting to get heavier the longer they kept going on this subject.

"Yes, I know the man." West nodded. "Or rather *of* the man. He is one of my father's clients. Like Tammy, I've never actually met him. All his business is done via email or through his personal assistant."

"That's not very helpful right now," Maria pointed out.

Tammy saw the suspicion in Maria's eyes as she looked from West to Tammy and knew it was more than just about Grayson. Maria knew something was going on between Tammy and West. Guilt heated her body like a fire burning through her veins in the form of a hot flush. Tammy hadn't had a hot flush in a whole year. Not wanting Maria to see her breaking into a cold dishonest sweat, Tammy moved out of her eyesight, trying to get as close to the door as possible. Maybe Maria would think she was checking out the horses.

"Oh, no." Maria looked up out of the front window to where Greg was still standing with his arms in the air. She had her phone held up. Tammy's hot flush was quickly replaced by a bucket of icy reality. They all watched the small dot representing Maggie moving through the house and fear rushed through her. "They're moving Maggie."

"In which direction?" West asked her. "Towards the front or the back of the house?"

"To the back?" Maria's brows were once again tightly drawn together in confusion as she glanced around at West. "Wouldn't they be moving her to the front of the house if they wanted to use her as leverage?"

"I would think so," Tammy said, a little startled at the thought of where they may be pushing the child. The back of the house was a cliff.

Tammy's head turned towards the cabin as more fear rose

inside her, thinking of that scared ten-year-old girl. Her first instinct was to jump out of the car and go charging in there like a raging mother grizzly bear tracking down her cubs. But Tammy knew that was only fear and anxiety clouding her rational thought.

"What's wrong?" the man in the house shouted to Greg. "Cat got your tongue?" He guffawed.

That is definitely Samuel! Tammy would recognize that silly laugh and dumb sense of humor anywhere. What she didn't understand was how he and his brother Pete had become tangled in with criminals. They were both gentle souls that wouldn't hurt a fly. Well, at least they used to be, when Tammy was younger. She tried to once again crane her neck to get a better glimpse of the window where the rifle was sticking out from.

"No, but I think you know that I can't give you Grayson." Greg shook his head. "But if you give me Maggie, we'll leave Montana. I'm sure your boss will like that."

Shock at Greg's words resounded through Tammy like she just stood on an electric eel in a river. A few words in Greg's offer had affected her that way. The first being that he was going to leave Montana. Which was ludicrous, because Tammy would love nothing more than for him to go and leave her hometown. She'd had enough drama as of late to last her a few lifetimes and was still sorting through a lot of the debris left by it. Tammy did not need more drama in her life, and that is what Greg Watson was; a big, crater-sized, earth-quaking, soul-shattering drama!

Chapter Seven

HER BROTHER'S HOUSE GUEST

"What do you think Greg means by that?" Maria looked around at West. Her eyes were filled with questions. "You don't think Greg knows who's behind all this trouble, do you?"

"I couldn't say." West shrugged. "I'm not from around here, and I hardly know any of these people. The only people I know are the Sparrows, your family, and the Parkers."

Tammy noticed that West left Greg and the Becketts off his list of known people in the area. He glanced at her, and she could see his eyes had darkened with the same distaste about lying that she had at this moment. Tammy was still uncertain as to why there was so much secrecy shrouding them at the moment about certain people, but she was going to find out. It was another note she added to the other mental notes she'd made throughout the day.

"He's not someone you should trust," Tammy piped up, wanting Maria to know not to put any faith in Greg Watson. He was sure to let you down and then turn on you like a viper. "I wouldn't be surprised if he was actually involved in this trouble somehow."

"Why don't you like him?" Maria's eyes caught and held Tammy's.

Tammy could see this was not the only question Maria had for her, but now was not the time to answer them. Especially when West seemed to be wanting to keep their relationship as well as all his other friendships a secret for some reason. Tammy was sure that involved Greg Watson. That man seemed to have a way about him that made those who knew him protect him in whatever manner they could.

"We have a lot of history," was all Tammy could say for now, although she was dying to blurt the truth out even if it made her look like a fool all over again. At least everyone would know the truth about the man. "All I will say is that he doesn't care who he has to walk over or destroy to get what he wants."

Tammy's eyes collided with West's startled ones, but he quickly recovered when he saw Maria's attention turn to him. He gave an uncomfortable laugh.

"Come now, Tammy, don't be so harsh on the guy. His daughter is trapped inside there with who knows how many men holding her hostage. He's going to be on edge." West clicked his fingers as if something had just dawned on him. "I think Greg worked for a private security firm that handled Cat's security for a while."

"He did?" Maria and Tammy said together.

Tammy looked at West quizzically, trying to see if he was once again embellishing the truth or if he was actually telling the truth. If so, it was a frightening one thinking of Greg Watson in private security.

"I'm sure he did," West said, squinting out the window at Greg. "I'll get my assistant to dig up the files on the firm, but I think he went on to run security for Grayson Wyatt."

"That would be interesting to know," Maria said, turning her attention back to Greg. "How do we tell him that Maggie's been moved to the back of the cabin?"

Tammy's eyes narrowed as she looked at West. Her thoughts on his sterling character were slowly becoming tarnished, and it was all because of West's loyalty to the man outside. Other than smartly maneuvering the truth around like any skillful lawyer would do, West didn't outright lie. As soon as you threw Greg Watson into the mix, West was spewing them out like a broken candy corn machine.

"Blow the horn," Tammy suggested, unable to surpass a small smile thinking if nothing else it would scare the bejeebers out of Greg.

"That might spook the man with the rifle pointed at us." Maria bit her lip and once again looked at the phone in her hand with worried eyes. "They haven't moved Maggie again. She is still at the back of the cabin."

"Do you think they are planning to make a run for it out the back?" Tammy asked, once again feeling a little alarmed by that thought.

Before Maria could answer her, all eyes once again turned back to look at Greg outside the vehicle when Samuel called back to Greg.

"Just spoke to the boss," the man called through the window once again. "No deal." He snarled. "It's either Grayson or your daughter."

Oh great! Tammy thought. That idiot Samuel just poked the huge, big grizzly bear named Greg. She watched Greg's posture stiffen ever so slightly, warning her that he had an eye on his prey and was tired of playing with it. Greg was about to go in for the kill. Samuel either knew just how Greg would react to that or was about to become grizzly bear meat. Tammy didn't know if she could watch the next bit of this scene unfold. It was like sitting at the movies, sinking down in your chair, knowing what was going to happen, but you just couldn't look away.

"I'm not leaving here without my daughter," Greg warned the man. His voice had dropped by a fraction that not everyone would notice, but Tammy was trained to pick up on the slightest nuisances or movements. "Your boss had one shot at getting rid of me and my family for good. If he wants to carry on hunting for ghosts, he can do so. I won't be any part of that."

Oh no! Tammy sighed inwardly, getting ready to duck down and cover her eyes.

"You seem to forget that we have your daughter," the man reminded him. "Wasn't losing everything else you held dear enough for ya?"

What did Samuel mean by that? Tammy's eyes were drawn back to Greg, wondering what everything he'd lost was. A distant memory started to try to swim its way through her crowded mind. *They lost everything in some sort of freak storm, Tam. I still think that, while the storm may have done damage, there was some sabotage involved.*

Please, please, no! Tammy pinched the bridge of her nose. *Please, Brian, don't tell me it's him?* She had silently pleaded with her brother, hoping that wherever he was, he was listening and would send her a sign to say it wasn't true.

I've offered him and his family a place to stay until he's on his feet.

A few weeks after Brian's death, Tammy had wanted to hire someone to run the ranch, but Constance had told her that Brian had left that friend he was helping out in charge, and things at the ranch were running as smooth as clockwork.

Now it all made sense. Tammy had still been in a such state of shock that she hadn't even asked who it was. She'd trusted Constance, and even though she'd spoken to her many times after that, the subject had never come up again. Tammy's throat suddenly felt dry, and her eyes widened as she looked at the back of Greg's head. Not only had been one of the first people she'd run into on her first day home, but he was living in her house! Tammy's mind was in such a spin over her revelation that she nearly missed what happened next.

"I don't have the power to resurrect someone who no longer exists," Greg hissed. "Nor do I have the time or patience to stand here trying to prove I'm not some sort of wizard." He turned and glanced back at Maria, giving her a slight nod. "So, you have two options here. Either you hand over my daughter peacefully and we leave without alerting anyone to your whereabouts. Or you may start enjoying your last few minutes of freedom."

Tammy watched Maria use her phone to send a message.

"Buddy, I'm the one with the rifle pointed at your head and a dozen men surrounding you," Tammy heard the overconfidence in Samuel's voice and knew he was about to get the surprise of his life.

"Are you sure about that?" Greg asked him, dropping his hands and folding them across his chest as a shot rang out once again, making her and Maria jump.

"What the..." Maria, who, like Tammy, had ducked down slightly slowly raised her head to watch the scene before them unfold like a weird dream.

The front door of the cabin burst open and a whole lot of men with their arms pinned behind their backs were marched out of the house. Tammy turned her head from side to side as she heard the crunch of shoes on the dried leaves. More men were being led out in the same way from the surrounding trees. A smile lifted Tammy's face when she noticed Ryan Beckett along with another cowboy who looked vaguely familiar to her had come to lend a hand. Tammy and Maria's heads swiveled back towards the cabin, both holding their breath as they waited for one or two more people to emerge from the cabin. Both women breathed a sigh of relief when Zac appeared to march Pete out. He was carrying a young girl with dark hair in his arms. As soon as they both spotted Greg, Zac put her down gently, and she flew down the stairs and was met halfway by her father who scooped her up into his strong arms.

Tammy smiled, fighting back tears in her misty eyes when she noticed Maria's were sparkling with unshed tears. It was truly a sight to behold, Greg Watson clinging to his daughter as if his life depended on it.

Tammy, Maria, and West climbed out of the car and walked to join the group gathering around Greg and Maggie. A few seconds later, the emergency vehicles arrived with blaring sirens and flashing lights. Without warning, and out of nowhere, tormenting flashes of another night she'd walked into the foray of fires and lights flashed through her mind. A pain so bad it knocked the breath from her nearly brought her to her knees.

Tammy squeezed her eyes shut, clenching her fists so tightly that her long nails drew blood from the palm of her hands. As the panic and terror that had clawed at her started to abate, she slowly opened her eyes relieved because she stood more to the back and out of the way no one had noticed the episode that had nearly dropped her to the ground. That was until her eyes collided with the green-gold ones she'd been trying to avoid the most. Something flashed in their depth but was gone before she could figure out what it was, and his attention was drawn away.

"This is a mess I'll gladly leave for the authorities to deal with," Maria told Cat and Chelsea as they watched animal control start to take stock of the animals that had been stolen.

"I couldn't agree with you more," Cat said. "I did see some of Four Lakes' cattle there."

"I also seen three of my horses." Chelsea turned to watch animal control scanning some of the horses. "Thank goodness for chipping."

"I'm so glad you're going to recover some of your animals, Chelsea." Maria's head turned when Greg called her name.

"Excuse me," Maria moved away from them and walked closer to Greg and Maggie.

Tammy watched Maria move towards Greg and Maggie as she tried not to let the lights and sirens get to her once again. She didn't need those green judgmental eyes assessing her again.

"Maggie, this is Maria," Greg introduced Maggie and Maria. Tammy was amazed to hear how gentle and loving his voice was. She had to press her nails once again into the palm of her hands as she pushed a long-lost memory back into its dark recess. "She's the lady..."

"That helped me on the radio," Maggie finished the sentence and threw her arms around Maria, giving her a big squeeze. "Thank you so much for answering my call and finding my phone."

"Speaking of your phone," Maria gave Maggie one last squeeze before stepping back and pulling the sparkling pink phone from her pocket. "I believe this belongs to you."

"Thank you." Tammy saw Maggie breathe a sigh of relief as she took her phone from Maria. Then she turned with a gleeful smile to her father, saying smugly, "See, Dad, I told you this watch wasn't just a fashion accessory or the latest must-have teen item. It's a necessity in today's uncertain and dark world."

"That's a bleak outlook on the world, and you don't have to convince me it was a good buy." Tammy felt her rebellious heart do a flip when Greg's face softened even more, and a genuine heartfelt laugh escaped his lips while he mussed the top of his daughter's hair. "I'm really happy to have bought it for you right now."

"I guess we should get moving," Zac said. "I want to get back to Brett and the others at the fire site."

"I'll come with you," West said.

"The three of us will drive with the two of you," Maria looked over at Greg. "Greg, do you mind taking my pickup back for me? You could drop off Tammy. I'm sure she wants to get home after a long flight from LA, the drive from Billings, and then all this drama."

She looked apologetically at Tammy, who had frozen on the spot at Maria's suggestion and looked at her horrified. Tammy was not ready to be left alone with Greg Watson and was about to ask if she could sit in the back of the truck.

"Are you Brynn's Aunt, Tammy?" Maggie smiled up at Tammy.

"Yes, I am," Tammy couldn't help but smile back at the pretty ten-year-old in front of her. She'd been through an ordeal, but still used her manners and managed to give Tammy a genuine smile. "You know Brynn?"

That was a stupid question, Tammy said to herself irritably. Of course, Maggie knew Brynn. If her memory served her correctly and they were the ones staying at the ranch, they'd have been there for almost a year now. Her heart felt heavy for a moment, wondering why Brynn hadn't mentioned Maggie and her dad over the past six months. Tammy immediately squashed that thought from her mind. Brynn had other things going on. Why would she say anything to Tammy? How would she know the bad history between Tammy and Greg?

"Yes, we've been living on Double A for over a year now," Maggie told her.

At least someone was being forthright with the truth today.

"Oh," Tammy said. "Well, then I'm sure Brynn is going to be super excited to see you after being away for all these months."

"How is she doing?" Maggie's face dropped and sadness darkened her pretty eyes.

"She's getting better," Tammy gave Maggie a warm smile and her voice softened even more. "Thank you for asking."

"And how are you doing?" Maggie's eyes looked up at her with such compassion and concern that Tammy's heart felt like it was going to explode, and tears stung the back of her eyes.

No one, except her Uncle Robert, had asked her that, especially not with such genuine heartfelt interest. It took every shred of strength Tammy could muster to swallow down the burning lump in her throat as she smiled down at Maggie.

"I'm getting there," Tammy said softly for Maggie's ears only. "That was very special and kind of you to ask."

"I'm sorry, I didn't mean to upset you," Maggie assured her. "I guess you've been asked that a lot lately."

"No, sweetheart," Tammy's voice grew hoarse with emotion as she crouched down in front of Maggie. "Not as much as you might think. And you didn't upset me at all. You can ask me anything you want."

Tammy was not expecting what Maggie did next. The young girl threw her arms around Tammy's neck and hugged her tightly.

"I'm so sorry about Uncle Brian and Aunty Lynn," Maggie's voice trembled. "They were my guardians in case anything happened to daddy."

"I'm sorry for your loss too, honey," Tammy whispered, her arms instinctively circling the child's small waist as she hugged her back.

When Tammy gently let Maggie go, her eyes once again

collided with Greg's narrowed, disapproving ones. Tammy ignored him and stood up, letting Maggie take her hand.

"Daddy, Aunt Tammy, and Brynn are back home," Maggie said, smiling up at Greg. "Will you sit in the back with me?" She looked at Tammy pleadingly.

"Sure," Tammy said, giving Greg a tight smile before letting Maggie drag her towards Maria's pickup truck.

When they climbed into the back of the vehicle, Tammy made sure that Maggie's seatbelt was secured before securing her own. She also chose to ignore Greg when he climbed into the driver's seat.

"So, I'm playing chauffeur this afternoon, I see." Greg grinned at his daughter but didn't look at Tammy.

"Daddy used to be a security detail for some celebrities," Maggie explained to Tammy. "This is how he used to drive them around."

"Oh, so he was also a chauffeur then?" Tammy grinned at Maggie.

Her eyes caught Greg's in the mirror. His were shooting daggers at hers. She simply smiled sweetly and turned her attention back to Greg's delightful child.

"Brynn told me that you know lots of celebrities because you work with them," Maggie looked at Tammy, fascinated. "What are they like? Daddy says most of them are spoiled and pampered like little brats."

"Oh, yes, they can be." Tammy made an animated face as she spoke to Maggie. "But some of them are just like you and me. Down to earth, kind, caring, and just trying to do their best for their families."

"Will you tell me who all the people you know are one day, please?" Maggie suppressed a yawn as the pickup bounced gently along the gravel drive heading for the ranch house.

"Sure," Tammy promised, watching as Maggie's eyes started to droop. She rested her head on Tammy's shoulder before drifting off.

Tammy smiled down at Maggie, adjusting her arm to wrap

around her small shoulders so the girl would be more comfortable. The poor little thing had gone through one heck of a traumatic experience today; it was only natural that she was exhausted. The car fell into an awkward silence once Maggie had drifted off to sleep, but Tammy preferred that to having to talk to Greg. She turned her head and stared out at the land that she hadn't seen in far too long. Even though Tammy was in a car with a man she disliked more than anyone else in the world, a feeling of peace once again settled over her as the land welcomed her back into its fold.

When they got back to the ranch house, Brynn and Amy burst through the back door to race towards the pickup.

"Hey, sleepyhead," Greg leaned over the seat and gently shook Maggie's leg. "We're home."

Home! The word sent shock waves once again crashing through Tammy. She didn't think she'd ever get used to Greg calling her house his home. Tammy glanced down at Maggie who stretched and forced her heavy lids open.

"I'm so tired, daddy," Maggie said sleepily. "Please, can you carry me to bed?"

"Of course, sweet pea," Greg's voice was all soft and gentle.

Tammy couldn't stay in close proximity to him any longer. She needed to get some space. Luckily Double A was a large ranch house. Hopefully, Constance or Brian had the sense to put Greg in the guest wing, which was on the other side of the family wing.

When Tammy climbed out of the pickup, Brynn along with three barking bassets hurtled towards her, nearly knocking her over when they pounced on her. As usual, Brynn's arms clamped around Tammy's waist like a vice grip as she clung to her.

"Hey, superstar," Tammy said gently, hugging her back and kissing her soft hair. "I'm home."

"I was so worried," Brynn's voice sounded shaky like she was about to burst into tears.

"I'm sorry I worried you, honey," Tammy said patiently. "But look who we brought back."

Tammy turned them to show her Maggie being gently lifted out of the car by Greg.

"Hello, Uncle Greg," Brynn waved at him but kept close to Tammy. "April, Craven, and Derby were worried too."

"I was worried too," Amy piped up from behind the excited dogs.

"Thank you, Amy." Tammy gave her a warm smile. "You know what, after all that action, I'm starving."

Tammy held her crowd back while Greg took Maggie into the house to take her to her room to have some sleep.

"Is Maggie, okay?" Brynn asked, wide-eyed as she watched them disappear into the kitchen.

"Yes, honey, she is absolutely fine. She is just very tired from all the stress and excitement." Tammy kept her one arm around Brynn, walking back into the house.

"Did I hear someone say they were starving?" Constance greeted them at the door. "I've just the thing for that. How about some tea and warm cherry pie?"

"If you have fresh whipped cream, count me in!" Tammy groaned in pleasure at the thought, and her stomach agreed with her by giving a soft growl.

G reg gently lay his sleeping daughter down on her bed. He pulled off her boots and covered her with the soft downy quilt Constance had given Maggie. Greg gave her a kiss on her forehead, smiling when she mumbled in her sleep, flipping over onto her stomach.

He couldn't believe it when he found out they were having another baby when they were in their forties. Greg was a bit worried about the pregnancy as his wife had not been well during its course. She'd also not been too pleased with the amount of time she'd had to take off from her work either due to the pregnancy.

Greg didn't like dwelling on Terri. She was no longer a part of his life and hadn't been for seven years now. The woman no longer bore his name, nor did she even take part in her kids' lives. Anger started to bubble up inside him at the thought of that selfish, spoiled woman. Greg took a deep breath. He never allowed himself to be angry around his kids. They'd had to endure enough of their mother's sullen moods when she was forced to spend time with them.

Greg quietly walked out of Maggie's room and pulled the door closed, leaving a small crack so he could hear if she called. He was at a bit of a loss as to what to do now that Tammy was home. The minute Greg had seen her, his gut had clenched, and he felt like he always did when he saw her. It was like there was a vice squeezing at his heart and cutting off the air to his soul. Greg and Brian had grown up together. Their grandfathers and fathers had been the best of friends.

Tammy had been Brian's kid sister that he dragged nearly everywhere with him. Greg had watched Tammy grow up. She'd always been a shy, reserved, kid with her nose in some book or other. That was when that same shy reserved little girl wasn't staring down an angry stallion to calm it or expertly roping a steer. Tammy had fascinated Greg from an early age. She had a wealth of knowledge in her head, could solve a complex math problem in a matter of minutes, and play the guitar like a rock star. Tammy could also sing, and dance, and she was the school's top gymnast. But the thing he admired the most about her was the way she rode. Greg gave a soft laugh, walking to his room, deciding to give Tammy and her guest some space to settle in. Greg sat down at the desk in his room to go through some ranch papers.

But memories of young Tammy Anderson kept stealing into his mind and distracting him. He remembered the first time he'd had her in his arms. It had been a few days before her seventeenth birthday. Greg's grandfather had a big white stallion with a pitch-black mane brought into the auction house. It was a thoroughbred. A highly-strung mean young stallion if ever there was one. All the grooms were petrified of the animal as it was not only wild, but also bigger than most thoroughbreds. The horse stood a good seventeen hands high.

If one good memory of Tammy stood out for Greg, it was that day in the auction house with that white devil of a horse. She'd stolen more than just his breath away with her astute handling of the frightening creature that day.

Chapter Eight
IN THE SHADOW OF A MEMORY – PART ONE

Brian and Tammy had come to look at Greg's grandfather's new auction horses with their father like they always did when new horses or cattle arrived. Tammy loved seeing all the horses and would spend as much time with each horse as she could. Neither the grooms nor Greg's grandfather minded. They would all comment how much calmer and easier to handle the horses were after she'd spent time with them. As a result, Tammy soon got the name of the Lewistown horse whisperer. While that nickname was revered by the ranchers, it got her terribly teased at school.

But that didn't seem to faze Tammy, who was pretty much a loner. The only person she hung around at school with was her best friend, Freddy Daniels and, on occasion, Maria Parker. Freddy's father owned the local pharmacy and was as big a bookworm as Tammy was. Greg gave himself a self-mocking laugh as he remembered that he'd actually been envious of the time nerdy Freddy got to spend with Tammy. How easy she was with him. Greg sighed and shook his head, thinking of one of the only reasons he ever attended the school dances or country shows was in hopes that Tammy would show. She rarely did, and when she did, Freddy or Maria were glued to her side like vicious guard dogs.

Greg even took an interest in his younger sister's showjumping so he could escort her to all the horse shows because Tammy was a show jumper. Her mother would take her to all her shows right up until she passed away. Then either her housekeeper, Constance, or her father would take her. Greg had come up with a brilliant idea to offer to take Tammy with him and his sister Tracy to a show one day when Tammy was having an issue with her family's timing.

Greg laughed, thinking of what a disaster that had been. He loved his younger sister, but she was not a very nice person and could be quite the mean and jealous girl. Tracy was also best friends with Bronwyn Brown, the school's queen bee, who detested Tammy and liked to make her the object of her ridicule as often as she could. Worse, Greg's brother and Bronwyn had this on-again-off-again relationship. When they were off, she loved to make a show of hanging onto Greg whenever she could. The day Greg took Tammy with his sister to the horse show, Bronwyn decided she wanted to come along to support her bestie. Bronwyn hated horses. The only reason she tolerated them was because of Greg's brother and his sister's love for them.

Greg put his head back and looked up at the ceiling fan in his room as he twirled his office chair from side-to-side, reminiscing about his teens and the disastrous horse show. Well, it had been for him, his sister, and Bronwyn. Tammy had once again shown her mettle and outshone everyone. She also did it with a grace that made everyone feel they were shining with her and had somehow helped her get to where she was. She also proved that class is not something you can buy, and no matter how pretty someone was on the outside, it still couldn't mask the ugly on the inside. Greg could still feel his chest puff up with immense pride when he'd seen the way Tammy had calmly and gracefully handled his sister and Bronwyn's bullying at the show. She'd stood looking at the two sneering girls with a soft smile on her beautiful face. Greg was about to interfere when Tammy started to walk away.

But Bronwyn had thrown one nastier jeer at her; she'd told Tammy that her ugly nag would never beat Tracy's thoroughbred mare. But he'd stopped himself when he'd seen Tammy sigh, shake her head, and turn back to face the two mean girls. Greg could still hear her soft, cool, calm voice that she did not raise once, her expression didn't even change.

"First, I have to correct your poor knowledge about horses. My horse is neither a small horse nor an old one, so she could not possibly pass as a nag. She is also one of only three thoroughbred horses here today. Tracy's horse, on the other hand, is fast approaching the age where her horse could be called a nag. Tracy's horse is also not one of the three thoroughbred horses here today. While her horse may be a gelded quarter horse, I'm quite sure he would not like to be referred to as a mare."

Tracy and Bronwyn had stood staring at Tammy in stunned silence. Tammy gave Tracy a big genuine smile and wished her the best of luck before complimenting her on her excellent horsemanship. When Tammy turned and glided off to get her horse, Greg had known for sure he'd lost his heart to the most special person in the entire world.

Greg blew out a breath. She was magnificent then, and much to his dismay, she was even more so now. Back then, she'd eye him out beneath those incredibly thick and long sooty black lashes, thinking he didn't notice. Tammy would blush whenever he talked to her or smiled at her, but she never timidly turned away. Nope, she met his stare head-on and then made him catch his breath each time she would give him that big smile. Greg sat up abruptly, giving his head a good shake, hoping to shake all thoughts of Tammy Anderson out of it.

Their relationship, if you could even have called it one, had ended with his heart being ripped open, exposing his aching, bleeding soul that had not been able to be saved. It had left a cold, empty space in its place and a badly wounded heart that had festered into a hard shell that had driven him through the rest of his life. It had shaped him into the hard, mistrusting man he'd become. The only people who'd ever been let into what was left of the love inside him were his kids. He grimaced; no wonder Terri had left him for another man. Terri might have been narcissistic and self-centered, but she still had a moderately warm heart. To give Terri her dues, she'd been happy to settle for what Greg could give her in the marriage. Stability, a family, and loyalty.

Of course, he'd cared for her, but the L-word wasn't something he'd ever said outright to her. Once again, the only people he'd ever been comfortable saying that word to again were his kids. Oh, and his parents. While he loved his irresponsible brother and awful sister, he didn't like them much. They had proven time and time again that they couldn't be counted on or trusted. If it came right down to it, the only person Greg really trusted was Brian. He closed his eyes and felt a burning slice through him as he thought of his best friend. It had been six months since that accident in Aspen, but Greg still had difficulty believing Brian and Lynn were gone.

While Greg had thought he'd still have a small part of them because he was Brynn's guardian, Tammy's lawyers neatly informed him that there was no document supporting his claim. Tammy had been named Brynn's guardian and would be taking responsibility for her. How Greg had itched to go up against that. He'd had the papers Greg and Lynn had drawn up by Ashley Cuthbert, but Ashley had advised him against it. Tammy was not someone he wanted to go up against in court. She had endless resources and one of the best law firms in the country representing her. Greg had a fast-declining business, thanks to all this trouble going on around Lewistown surrounding ranches. He was also living on a ranch that was now rightfully Tammy's.

Greg slammed his fist on the desk as hot anger bubbled up inside once again. Greg shouldn't be in this position, and he still couldn't believe he was. His eyes fell on the stacks of paper piling up on his desk, knowing he had to get through them today. Greg was meeting his son, Will, tomorrow to discuss his plans to help get Watson's Farm Store and Auctions back on track. They had had to put the house renovations on hold to pump capital into restoring the business. Greg's anger started to bubble over when he thought of how his selfish sister and her new man had run the business into the ground. They were using it as their personal ATM. Tracy had nearly popped a gasket when their grandfather had finally passed away at the age of ninety-nine. He'd left everything to Greg and not even a penny to Tracy or their brother.

Well, his brother and grandfather had apparently discussed the will at length. His brother was in no need of an inheritance. Their grandfather knew Greg's brother was never interested in the family business. Tracy wasn't really either. All she wanted from it was the money it made, not caring that most of it always got put back into the business to keep it going. Both Greg's brother and grandfather had determined that Tracy had already more than spent her share of her inheritance. That was when Greg's grandfather had changed his will to leave everything to Greg, and his brother had co-signed it. In a fit of rage, Tracy had warned him that it wasn't over and that she'd get her share of the business one way or the other. That was over eight years ago. She'd disappeared, never to be heard of again, along with that low-life husband number four of hers. Greg sighed once again, trying to clear thoughts of his family and Tammy from his mind.

Greg sat forward and started to sort out the papers in front of him. But as he stared at his laptop screen, he found his mind drifting back to the first time he'd held Tammy.

THIRTY-SIX YEARS AGO

The new white stallion had only just arrived at the auction house when Tammy, Brian, and their father showed up. The moment Tammy had seen the white horse with the unusual coloring, she'd flown over to him. Tammy's father had gone with Greg's grandfather. Brian had snuck off to go see his latest girlfriend, leaving

Greg to keep an eye on Tammy around the horses. After saying goodbye to Brian and promising to cover for him, Greg had gone to find Tammy and had gotten such a fright.

Greg watched in horror, frozen to the spot for a few seconds, with his heart trying to jump out of his body through his throat. Tammy was scaling the wooden fencing to jump over the top and into the stallion's stall without an iota of fear. As she shoved one leg and was about to maneuver the other over the edge, Greg sprang into action. He rushed over to her, plucking her small frame from the fence. He'd been acting on pure instinct and had not expected her to turn angrily in his arms before he managed to pull her on the ground.

The movement made him lose his balance. They toppled backward onto the ground with Tammy on top of him and his arms holding her firmly against him. Her angry blue eyes leveled with his as she pushed herself up onto her hands. Her porcelain cheeks were aflame with outrage, and her mass of golden-blond hair was threatening to break loose of its elastic band confines. Greg was expecting the full force of the fury burning in her eyes to lash out at him. But then their eyes locked.

The blazing fire burning in the deep blue depths of her eyes started vanishing as her pupils dilated, and she stared at him as if she was mesmerized. It was the first and last time in his life that he'd actually felt the world around him start to fade as he got lost in her eyes. The urge to kiss her was so strong it almost overwhelmed him, and his lips started to move towards hers. Not wanting to take his eyes from hers, he watched her head slowly start to descend to his as she followed his lead. A great thundering crash against the wooden fence yanked him painfully back to reality.

They still hadn't broken eye contact and lay there staring at each other in half shock, half anticipation. Their large white chaperone decided it was time to step up his separation tactics, rearing up and flying out his top hooves in warning. The horse started to rear up and kick at its stall as if objecting to Greg holding Tammy. Suddenly Greg knew his best friend Brian would most definitely not approve of him holding his little sister. At the thought of Brian, Greg flew to his feet, accidentally shoving Tammy off him. She fell back and nearly hit her head on the fence. Greg jumped forward, holding out his hand to help her up, but she slapped it away.

"I can get up by myself!" Tammy hissed. The hurt that flashed in her eyes for a few seconds was like a stake through his heart. She jumped to her feet, and the hurt was gone. She glared at him, her eyes once again burning blue flames of anger. "Are you trying to knock me out?"

She didn't bother to dust herself off. Spinning around, her attention was drawn back to the great beast who'd instantly settled the minute Tammy had stood up. The horse's big black eyes seemed to bore into Greg, its ears pulled back warningly. Greg stood, his chest rising and falling as if he'd just run a race, while his heart pumped hard against his ribs. But he ignored the big brute as he stood. He was too stunned by his reaction to being so close to Tammy.

The minute Greg had touched Tammy, an electric current had shot through him, fusing her into his heart and carving her image into the space reserved for his soul mate. He'd know without a shadow of a doubt that if he'd kissed her, he'd never want to kiss anyone else. The thing that had scared Greg the most was that the look in her eyes mirrored the feelings spiraling through him, weaving invisible emotional threads around them, drawing them together as their soul started to be stitched into the fabric of time; they were fated to be soulmates.

But as with everything touched by fate, only so much is clear; the rest is scattered into a person's future like puzzle pieces being turned over in no particular order. Greg felt as if he'd just turned over a good few pieces but still none of them quite fit just yet. He held back a shudder, knowing that before today he'd still had a chance to walk away from her. Although there were a lot of pieces to choose from, there were only ever two outcomes in life. You either won, or you lost, and Greg knew deep down that he was heading for a world of pain somewhere along the line.

But he had to walk this path now that his heart had chosen, and his soul had approved the choice.

Greg stood, staring at Tammy, watching her intently. She'd always shown the promise of becoming a beautiful woman. Greg was sure, however, that no one ever expected just how beautiful she'd become — She was breathtaking. That was one of the reasons most of the girls and boys at their school were so mean to her. Tammy, however, seemed totally oblivious to her looks, which made her even more alluring, and unfortunately, the target of the mean schoolgirls' hateful jealousy. It didn't help that Tammy was also kind, talented, intelligent, gentle, and fiercely brave. As she was currently displaying as she once again swung herself up to perch onto the wooden fence. Both her long jeans-clad legs hung down in front of her as she balanced perfectly and started to talk in a soft, soothing voice to the stallion.

He smiled, knowing that one of the biggest mistakes most of the bullies at school made was underestimating her, or mistaking her shyness for timid weakness. Tammy was far from weak or timid, and not afraid to stick up for herself or others in need. The girl stood up to some of the fiercest horses Greg had seen and managed to tame their wild souls without any force. Other than the force of her iron will and her fierce love of the mystical intelligent creatures. Storm Front snorted, and Greg suddenly realized he'd walked forwards towards where Tammy was balanced on the wooden fence.

"Stay back!" Tammy hissed at Greg, not bothering to turn her head. "You've caused him enough stress."

"Don't expect me to leave you here alone with him," Greg told her in no uncertain terms but moved back to give her a bit more space to calm the horse.

"Fine, do what you must, but stay back." Tammy's voice was stern and commanding, but it totally changed to soft and cooing when she spoke to the stallion. "What's your name?"

"Storm Front," Greg supplied for her.

"I can read!" Tammy's ponytail flicked when she turned her

head to glare at him. "Can you be quiet, please? I'm establishing a rapport with him."

"Sorry," Greg said, lowering his voice.

For the next few minutes, he stood holding his breath, forcing himself to stand still and not rush forward every time Tammy reached out her hand to the great white beast in front of her. After about five minutes, she achieved what the Storm Front's owners had said no one had yet achieved. The horse walked forward and touched his nose to Tammy's hand.

"There you go," Tammy gave another soft laugh. "You are so beautiful and misunderstood, aren't you?" Another laugh escaped her lips as the horse gave a nod as if he understood her. "That's okay because I understand you."

The horse stepped closer to her and nudged her. Greg once again nearly had a heart attack when Tammy nearly lost her balance but quickly and skillfully recovered without falling off the fence.

"Cheeky." Tammy laughed. "You can smell the treats in my pocket, can't you?"

Storm Front snorted and nodded his head, showing his teeth. It was as if the blasted horse was grinning.

"Ah, so you're a clown, are you?" Tammy's throaty laughter bubbled up inside as she rubbed the stallion's head. "Okay, I'll give you a piece of an apple."

Tammy reached into one of the many pockets on her hiking vest and pulled out a quartered slice of an apple. She held it out to him, and, to Greg's surprise, Storm Front gently took it from her hand. From what Greg read, most of the stable hands and the horse's previous owner dropped the treat or food on the ground and ran. Storm Front was a notorious biter and didn't like people in his face.

Greg's heart nearly stopped when the next thing Tammy did was slide off the fence into the beast's stall. He was about to rush over but stopped when Tammy held her hand up, indicating for him to keep still.

"You don't mind standing here, do you, big boy?" Tammy said

soothingly, carefully reaching up to rub his large, white neck. "When was the last time you had a good brushing?"

Greg thought his lungs were going to explode. He'd held his breath for so long and forced his feet to stay where they were.

"I'm going to reach over this way and get your brush. Is that okay?" Tammy rubbed his neck, keeping him calm with one hand and hooking his brush with the other.

Storm Front didn't look phased at all. He moved his head and shook out his great black mane, and his skin quivered as Tammy started using the brush. She ran the brush over the same path she'd run her hand on his neck.

"That feels good, doesn't it?" Tammy's throaty laugh once again rumbled up from her chest and squeezed his heart.

As if on cue, Storm Front gently snorted and gave a slight shake of his head but didn't move.

"Good boy," Tammy got braver and hooked her other arm around his neck as she trailed the brush down his powerful leg muscle but still Storm Front didn't fidget or try to bolt.

"Am I really seeing this?" Tammy's father's voice made Greg jump.

He'd been so engrossed in watching Tammy work her magic on one of the meanest, ill-tempered horses he'd ever seen without so much as breaking a sweat.

"That horse hasn't let anyone get that close to him in years," Greg's grandfather said, quietly coming up beside them.

"I still want to rush over there and yank my daughter out of that stall," Garth Anderson said softly, not wanting to startle the horse.

"I wouldn't do that," Greg said, looking at Tammy's father. "I tried that, and Storm Front went berserk. The minute Tammy walked up to him; I think he claimed her as his human."

"That's a strange thing to say," Sam Watson, Greg's grandfather, frowned at his grandson. "But I think I understand what you mean." His eyes were drawn back to the thin golden-haired girl gently brushing the stallion that all but dwarfed her. "If your daughter can capture a beast like Storm Front, Garth," the age lines at the side of his light blue eyes crinkled, "I have to say I now feel even more sorry for the poor man who loses his heart to her."

"I feel sorry for myself, having to fight those poor fools off," Garth breathed. "I knew she looked a lot like her mother but..." He shook his head, his eyes misted over as they always did when he thought of his late wife.

"You never expected her to blossom into what society would have called an unrivaled beauty in another bygone era?" Maria Parker's voice had then all turn to her as she stood there, grinning at them.

"Hello, young lady," Sam greeted her. "I see you're still rotting your mind reading those historical romance novels."

"Well, then you can blame your wife for that, Uncle Sam." Maria laughed cheekily. "She's the one who gave me my first historical romance."

"I told her not to read that book to you as a bedtime story that time we looked after you and your brother," Sam tutted, shaking his head. "After that, you plagued her night and day to read you more."

"I miss Daisy," Maria's voice dropped.

"I do too, love. I do too." Sam smiled sadly at Maria. "Is your grandmother here with you?"

Greg noticed a light in his eyes as he craned his neck to look behind Maria.

"Yes, she's back there looking at those 'mangy calves' you have in stock." Maria laughed, watching Sam's eyes slit.

"Well, I never!" Sam excused himself and sauntered off, looking at Maria's grandmother mutter beneath her breath. "Mangy? The audacity of that old crone."

"Is there something going on between our grandparents?" Greg said, frowning.

Maria shrugged and turned her attention to Tammy grooming Storm Front.

"He's magnificent," Maria breathed.

"He's a beast that my daughter is trying to tame, and I have a dreadful feeling she's found her birthday present." Garth shook his head, folding his arms across his chest as he watched his daughter.

"I think you might just be right, Uncle Garth," Maria agreed with him. "Tammy had that same look when she met Snapper."

"Please don't remind me," Garth rolled his eyes. "Her mother nearly never spoke to me again when we came home with that brute on Tammy's tenth birthday."

"She loved Snapper," Maria said softly. "Her heart was broken after his fall."

"I know!" Garth sighed, running his hand through his thick hair. "But I think this demon is ten times worse than Snapper ever was."

"I'll help her with him," Greg offered quickly.

"That's kind of you, son," Garth smiled appreciatively at Greg. "But I have a feeling that horse will only let Tammy near him."

"I read his chart," Maria told him. "He was in a car accident when he was three years old. His previous owners were transporting him to their new ranch."

"Yes, the horse box caught alight, and he nearly didn't get out." Greg continued the story. "Since then, he's been a nightmare to handle and won't let anyone get close to him."

"Well, they do get close to him," Maria pointed out. "But there are always injuries in the process."

"He is from an excellent thoroughbred lineage." Garth tilted his head to the side, sousing out the horse. "His mother is one of the only pure white racehorses, and his father was another rare coloring being pure black."

"Yes." Maria's eyes lit up as she looked up at Garth. "I read that. If anything, he'd make a great horse to breed, Uncle Garth."

"Did you and my daughter plan this?" Garth looked at Maria teasingly.

"No." Maria frowned. "I haven't spoken to Tammy in a day. I came here looking for her to ask her what she'd done for her birthday."

"I'm teasing you, honey," Garth mussed her hair, then sighed. "I guess I'd better go rescue Maria's grandmother and then ask your grandfather if he'll sell him to me?"

"I think he will," Greg assured Garth. "Everyone who works here was dreading having Storm Front on the auction block."

"I guess that's one good thing about the horse's foul temperament then." Garth gave his daughter and the horse one last look. "You'll keep an eye on her for me?" He looked Greg in the eye. "I see her brother has snuck off to see his latest conquest."

"Uh..." Greg suddenly felt like a deer caught between two oncoming trucks. He'd been so absorbed with Tammy that he'd completely forgotten Brian's cover story.

"Don't worry," Garth patted Greg on the shoulder. "I'll let my son know you stuck to whatever story the two of you came up with this time."

Garth laughed at the expression that Greg knew was one of shame for letting his best friend down.

"I'm going to go and look at the other new horses, leaving you to continue drooling over Tammy." Maria gave Greg a smug smile as his head shot around to look at her. "Don't worry. No one else knows, and your secret is safe with me."

Before Greg could find the words to say, Maria quietly walked away, leaving Greg to do his duty and watch out for Garth's daughter while she groomed the beastly horse.

A knock at Greg's door yanked from his memories. He looked down, and realized his hands were clenched in fists and his heart throbbed as if it were bruised in his chest.

"Not this time, Tammy Anderson!" Greg hissed under his breath, ruthlessly ignoring whatever message his body was trying to send him.

Never again would he allow that woman to get under his skin. *But it seems like she still is, or you never really managed to get her out from under it.*

"Shut up!" Greg said softly through gritted teeth to that annoying voice in his head. "You've done more than your fair share of damage to my life," he admonished his subconscious.

"Daddy?" Greg's heart lurched and immediately warmed when he heard the soft voice of his daughter.

"Hey, princess." Greg pulled the door open, and Maggie hurtled into his arms. "What's wrong, honey?" An alarm zinged through him like someone had zapped him with a taser.

"Please, can I stay with you?" Maggie buried her head in the crook of his neck with her arms wrapped tightly around his neck. Greg could feel her small body tremble.

"Of course, you can, princess," Greg said softly, cradling her gently in his arms and kissing her head.

Thoughts of Tammy Anderson and the dilemma he was in living at Double A were pushed aside, and another spurt of anger shot through him. Pete and that gang were really lucky they were currently locked up safely in prison. If they weren't, Greg would be hunting them down right now for daring to take his child and terrorizing her.

"Can we go get something to eat?" Maggie asked him, pushing her hands between them to keep her arms warm.

"Yes, we can," Greg told her and started walking out of his room towards hers. "But first, I think you need to get into something warm. You're freezing cold."

"Okay," Maggie nodded. "But will you stay by me?"

"I'm not going anywhere," Greg promised her.

His eyes narrowed as he watched his daughter grab something and slip into her bathroom. Maggie hadn't done this since she was three years old, the year her mother left. It had taken years before she was confident enough to sleep in her own room or go anywhere without him after that. Now here they were again. Those monsters had torn her confidence and made her fear again. Greg's hands clenched at his sides as he fought to get his anger under control before Maggie came out of the bathroom. Whatever it took, Greg was going to join in the ranch hunt to find who was behind all this, although Greg had an idea who it was after this afternoon.

"I'm ready, daddy," Maggie said, running out of the bathroom as if she'd been spooked.

Maggie clutched Greg's hand as they walked down to the kitchen to get some dinner. Maggie's usual banter and happy chatter that usually brightened the dinner table was missing that evening. Sadly, Greg knew it would be that for a while, which only made him angrier and more determined than ever. He'd do whatever it took to find the culprit that had stolen his daughter's joy, the one terrorizing their land.

Chapter Nine
BETRAYAL OF THE WORST KIND

It had been three days since Tammy had arrived home, and three days since the ordeal at Double A ranch. She'd been on edge since she'd arrived back in Montana, especially because it meant she had to live under the same roof as Greg Watson. Tammy had already fallen in love with Greg's daughter, Maggie. She'd only wished she could have Maggie there without her father.

Everywhere she went in her house or on the ranch she knew there was a good chance of bumping into him, which was exactly what happened at least four to five times a day. Tammy was waiting in her brother's study for Constance because she wanted to know where all the ranch's paperwork was. She wanted to go over it and then send it all to Uncle Robert to make sure everything was in order.

"You were looking for me, Tammy?" Constance walked into the study.

"Yes, where are all the ranch papers and books?" Tammy looked at Constance and noticed her cheeks got a red stain on them like they did when she knew conflict was brewing. "Constance?"

"I'm still not used to you being such a businesswoman, my child," Constance said, pride puffing up her chest. "You truly have become a remarkable woman. Your parents would be so proud of you."

"Thank you," Tammy said politely, trying to hang onto her patience with Constance's stalling, diverting tactics. "Constance, I have to get going to the Mountain Rise barbeque in an hour and I would really like to get the books."

"Oh, yes," Constance said with a nod as if she just remembered what Tammy had asked of her.

Tammy sighed, leaning back in the leather office chair. She raised her eyebrows expectantly, waiting for Constance to answer the question.

"They are in Greg's room," Constance told her. "He likes to go over all the paperwork and books up there because he doesn't want to invade the family's space. He feels this office belongs to you and Brian."

"Why does Greg have the ranch books?" Tammy's brows creased and her anger started to stir. "Why aren't they with the ranch foreman?"

"Because your uncle Robert called here six months ago and asked Greg to help out with them," Constance shocked Tammy by saying. "I thought Robert would've told you that."

"I'm afraid he forgot to mention it," Tammy leaned forward on her elbows, clasping her hands in front of her. "I would like them back on my desk by the time I get back from the barbeque this evening."

"I will ask him if he wouldn't mind letting you take a look at them," Constand said.

"Excuse me?" Tammy's brows drew tighter together. "If I can have a look at them?"

Tammy looked at Constance, her eyes narrowing. Ever since she'd gotten home, she'd felt there was something different about the housekeeper she'd known since birth. Now she was baiting Tammy for some reason. Constance might think she was playing the innocent by saying what she had. But Tammy knew a manipulation tactic when she saw one. Constance's gameplay here was amateurish compared to the celebrities she'd worked with.

"Tammy dear, please don't alienate Greg," Constance implored her. "It was so kind of him to step in and take over the running of the ranch until you returned."

"Alienate Greg?" Tammy's voice lowered to a dangerous level, and her eyes slit.

Was Constance seriously trying to make Tammy feel like Greg was the one being alienated here? Tammy was the one being stopped from seeing vital information about her ranch. Suddenly, images of how Martin had tried to stop Tammy from seeing information about their joined finances flittered through her mind. Or always tried to manipulate her into what to buy or not to buy hammered in her head. It had turned out he was hiding the fact that he'd drained that account and skillfully siphoning off their retirement nest egg. A nest egg she'd found out the year she'd caught him cheating on her only she'd been contributing to.

Looking at Constance now, she knew without a shadow of a doubt she too was hiding something, and that made her angry. Tammy was done with lies, secrets, dishonesty, and being betrayed. She'd learned the hard way you couldn't trust anyone, well except for her best friend Brenda and her Uncle Robert. Tammy had thought she could trust Constance, the woman had been more like a grandmother to her than a housekeeper. She had been there since the day she was born, running the Double A ranch house.

"For goodness' sake, Tammy. Don't go getting all up on that high horse with me, young lady!" Constance stood her ground. "You haven't been here in years, let alone drop by these last two months. I, for one, am really grateful Greg was here. How on earth would I have run the ranch?"

"I offered to send someone *I trusted*!" Tammy knew she was simmering on the edge of an explosion now as Constance just added more fuel to the growing anger inside her.

Other than Constance defending Greg as if he was her cub

there was something up with Constance. Tammy had noticed it the first day she'd arrived back home, but she'd put it down to everything that happened that day. Only ever since that day, Tammy had seen Constance snooping around, and the woman always seemed to be lurking in the shadows. Tammy could've sworn Constance had even eavesdropped on some of her conversations these past few days.

"I would not live here with a stranger running the place!" Constance raised her voice. Her weathered cheeks pinkened with anger as she admonished Tammy as if she was a naughty child. "Why don't you just leave the running of the farm to Greg? *He knows what he's doing!*"

That was it! Tammy felt the last vestiges of her control snap. Heat flooded through her veins in the form of burning anger. Ages of pent-up grieving, anger at Martin, and confusion over all the past months' events hit her like a tsunami of rage.

"Come inside and close the door behind you!" Tammy's voice was one of icy control daring Constance to try and defy her.

It took every ounce of control Tammy had not to let the tidal wave gaining strength and height inside of her burst out devastating everything in its path.

"I..." Constance's face went from angry pink to deathly pale. "I'm so sorry, Tammy." Her eyes widened at the look of Tammy's stormy blue eyes and the formidable set of her shoulders.

"If you knew what was good for you right now, you'd do exactly as I said," Tammy warned her. "If not, I will take that as your formal resignation with immediate effect."

"Tammy!" Greg's deep voice cracked like a lightning bolt through the highly charged atmosphere. "Leave Constance alone. What is this all about?"

"I..." Constance didn't take her eyes off Tammy as she stood caught between Tammy and Greg. Two people she was suddenly realizing were more formidable than she'd known. Her hands nervously toyed with her apron. "I'd better go and leave you two."

"You will do nothing of the sort!" Tammy could feel the rage pushing her onwards as she slowly rose from behind the desk. "You will come in here and take a seat." She pointed to the door. "Or walk through that door, pack your things, and carry on walking."

"I..." Constance didn't take her eyes from Tammy for one minute.

She felt Greg shift slightly as his shoulders stiffened. She glanced at him. He was now standing rigidly in the doorway. His eyes narrowed warily, watching Tammy. Constance knew instinctively that, like her, he'd never seen such a furious Tammy. She doubted even Greg knew Tammy had it in her.

Constance swallowed and slowly turned her head back to meet the icy cold stare of the woman she no longer recognized as the girl she'd help raise. Tammy stood looming in front of them like the proud, unemotional, unmovable mountain outlined in the background behind her. She radiated a kind of confidence Constance had never seen in the once shy, sweet little Tammy. Constance was so proud of how Tammy was standing her ground and defending her home, despite being petrified.

By the way Greg had gone quiet and was assessing the situation, Constance knew he'd deduced the same thing she had. He wasn't quite sure how to handle this version of Tammy. Outwardly, Tammy looked cool, calm, and in control. But both Constance and Greg knew there was a powder keg of anger with a lit fuse heading towards it. Constance had dreaded this day, but she'd know it would come. It was time to atone for what she'd done and face the chopping block. But she could also not live with the guilt of what her actions had caused.

Constance looked from Tammy to Greg, feeling the tension sizzling in the room and did the only thing she could. She walked into the office and sat down. She nearly jumped out of her skin when Greg was the first to break the highly charged silence.

"What is this all about?" Greg's voice was dangerously low as his and Tammy's eyes met.

"This is none of *your* business," Tammy warned him. "So, I suggest you turn around and leave, closing my office door behind you."

"No," Greg shook his head and walked into the office to pull up the chair next to Constance. "I'm staying!"

Greg knew he was antagonizing her and that he was not just poking a bear, but a very dangerous dragon that could very possibly burn both him and Constance to death. He could feel the fight for control Tammy was having inside herself. Greg also knew how angry she was. No, he'd rather call it fury. Tammy was burning with a fury he'd never seen in her before and he'd been on the wrong side of her anger once before. That had been bad enough and had nearly killed him. It did emotionally cripple him. But at least he could see just how angry she'd been as the flames had burned in her eyes.

The woman standing stiff, expressionless, and with cool emotionless eyes was a lot more dangerous. There was no way Greg could leave poor Constance to weather whatever storm Tammy was about to unleash on her alone. He was also curious as to what had brought Tammy to the point of losing control. Greg could only imagine it has something to do with him. That was yet another reason he would not leave Constance alone with a rage-filled Tammy. Greg was hesitant at first to seek Tammy out to discuss what should've been discussed with her as soon as she'd gotten home.

The big elephant that had been trying unsuccessfully to hide in every room he and Tammy crossed over the last few days. The fact that he and his daughter were living here. He also wanted to explain the reasons why they were here and why Brian had done what he did. But Greg knew that today was probably not going to be the day it got discussed. He, Tammy, and the girls were also supposed to be attending the barbeque at Mountain Rise. So, he needed some way to calm her down because it was crucial they both attended. Zac, Brett, and West had something they needed to discuss with all of them.

That's when Greg suddenly realized that Tammy also had no idea about the upcoming party or that they were supposed to be hosting celebrity guests at Double A. Greg knew now was also not the best time to bring that up unless he really did want to get blown away. His eyes immediately went to the three deadly katanas mounted on the office wall. They had been Brian's pride and joy after he managed to obtain them at an auction. Greg wondered if Tammy would erupt if he got up and quickly removed them from her sight. But his attention was drawn back to the cold smooth voice of Tammy.

"What are you doing?" Tammy asked him, staring down at him.

"Staying so you don't make a foolish mistake in a fit of rage," Greg told her knowing the instant his words left his lips that they were not the right ones to say.

At least he finally got a glimpse of just how angry Tammy was and really wished he'd had a chance to get those katanas. Because if ever he'd seen a red rage, that was what flashed in Tammy's eyes for a few seconds as they narrowed in on him. Images of Storm Front flashed through his head. Greg had seen the same fury in that horse's eyes.

Tammy had already been pushed beyond her limits and she couldn't remember a time in her life when she'd felt such rage burn through her. But no one was ever going to try and control or manipulate her life again. She also had no time for stubborn egotistical nosey cowboys who were lording themselves around *her* home.

"I think it's time you left." Tammy saw the shock of her words register in both Greg and Constance's eyes.

"Tammy, no," Constance said, her hand shooting out to Greg's arm for support.

Tammy saw Constance lean back and shrink before Tammy's icy stare.

"You've used up all your warnings," Tammy told her. "I'll have your retirement package and severances ready for you by the end of the day." Her eyes held the shock-addled ones of Constance.

"What?" Constance stammered as her eyes looked at Greg for help then flew back to Tammy's. "What on earth has come over you?"

"You're not going anywhere, Constance," Greg's eyes and voice softened when he put a protective hand on her shoulder. "And neither am I!"

Greg raised his eyes to meet Tammy's. She saw his slight flinch when he must have realized not only had he fed fuel to her already flaming rage, but he'd also just fanned it. Without a word, Tammy broke eye contact. Fighting to keep her hands from shaking from the force of her anger, she picked up her phone and found Robert's number.

"Hi, honey," Robert answered on the third ring.

"How quickly can you legally evict people from your ranch?" Tammy's eyes once again met Greg's. But instead of being panicked, his expression changed to one of confidence as if he knew something she didn't. At that look, Tammy knew she was missing a vital bit of information.

"Who are you wanting to evict?" Robert asked her.

"I'm going to ask you a question, Uncle Robert, and for once I expect an honest answer," Tammy said through gritted teeth, feeling the first prickles of hurt knowing that her uncle may have somehow betrayed her.

reg felt alarm spread through him like someone had spread ice water through his veins.
She doesn't know!

Greg swallowed as his heart started to pound and his mind spun trying to figure out why no one had told Tammy about what Brian had done. Then another thought struck him. Tammy was going to think he was the one who had wanted the truth kept from her. He and Tammy didn't have a good track record when it came to him keeping secrets from her. Greg had to get her to put the phone down from her uncle so he could tell her he'd thought she'd know.

But the minute her eyes had met his, he knew he had to act fast.

"Tammy, put the phone down, and we can talk this out calmly," Greg said softly.

"Greg Watson is a permanent fixture at *my* ranch?" Tammy turned her back on Greg, stepped around her office chair, and looked out the window.

It was too late. She'd already figured it was him who had kept what Brian had done from her.

"Uh..." Robert hesitated. "Look, Tammy, I wanted to tell you, but Constance and I both thought it would be better to do so once you were settled. You've been through so much already over these past three and a half years. Then all that drama happened on your first day, and you've had so much other stuff to sort out..."

Tammy was done with listening to excuses for other people's dishonest behavior. Her heart was pounding in her chest, and there was a roaring in her ears. Deep down she knew what Robert was about to tell her, or at least the gist of it.

"I'm going to give you ten seconds to start explaining," Tammy's voice was flat with a hint of warning.

"Tammy!" Robert said gently. "I can hear in your voice that you are enraged for some reason. Why don't you go ride that brute of a horse of yours that is arriving with Jude today?" He suggested. "I know how that always calms you down."

"You now have five seconds," Tammy ignored his unsolicited advice.

"Okay!" Robert sighed. "Brian asked me about a month before the accident if I could set up a clause in his will to give a quarter of his share of the ranch to Greg. I thought it was peculiar, so I asked Brian why. He also wanted to know if all his affairs were in order, so I asked him why he was so worried about it all of a sudden..."

"You're going off-topic," Tammy told him, coldly cutting into his explanation.

"Greg has a quarter of Brian's share of the ranch and Brynn gets the other three-quarters of it," Robert told her. "I'm sorry I didn't tell you, Tammy. You know I would never intentionally betray you."

"Just the ranch or everything on it as well?" Tammy once again ignored Robert's apology.

"It states that Greg gets a quarter of his share of the ranch house, the land, and the cattle," Robert informed her. "Look, once you've cooled down, as I know you're probably even more enraged now than you were before, we can talk about this more. But I think Brian thought someone was trying to kill him. He wanted to make sure Greg, Brynn, and ..."

"Have all my legal affairs sent over for the sole attention of Ashley Cuthbert in Lewistown, please," Tammy's voice was flat. "Include a report on Brian's state of mind when he asked you to do this and any reasoning you may have for it." She glanced out at the tall, majestic mountains rising in the distance and felt them slowly start to soothe the anger inside her. "I think it goes without saying from here on out that you and your firm no longer represent me or the Double A Ranch."

"Tammy, can we talk about this?" Robert's voice was laced with worry.

"Make sure everything is with Ashley by Monday at the latest." Tammy didn't wait for his reply and ended the call.

She stood staring out of the window, composing herself. Tammy fended off the pain of knowing the one person in this world she thought she could depend on, and trust had betrayed her. Her uncle had lied to her and had practically pushed her into another bad situation. Tammy's eyes traveled over the large stone structure standing proud and tall looming over the valley. It was unmovable and solid. Why couldn't people be that way? Solid, loyal, and dependable? She closed her eyes and drew in a long silent breath, willing back that burning hot feeling of anger. Because right now, Tammy had no use for this terribly painful feeling slicing through her aching heart from her uncle's betrayal.

"Tammy?" Constance's soft voice helped with that.

The instant she'd heard it, the anger sparked again. Constance was yet another person in her life to have betrayed her. What was wrong with people? Tammy straightened her shoulders and stepped back around the desk. Without a word, she sat back down in her chair, leaning back in it like the boss she was. No matter what Greg may think his share of this ranch entitled him to, she was still the major shareholder, which made her the boss. Tammy was not going to be walked over ever again. How dare anyone decide what was best for her or what she should or should not know about the things that affected her life. Especially now when it was no longer just her life she was responsible for but a little nine-year-old girl's too.

"I take it you both already know what Robert just told me?" Tammy looked accusingly from Greg to Constance.

"I can imagine," Constance's voice wobbled with uncertainty and a hint of fear. "I can explain why I didn't say anything to you." She quickly quieted down at Tammy's warning look.

"Tammy, I didn't know that no one had told you about what Brian did," Greg said quickly. "I thought you'd known when you arrived home."

"Of course, you did," Tammy's tone spoke volumes, letting Greg know she didn't believe a word he said.

Tammy didn't trust herself to continue with this conversation. She needed to put it on hold and think it over. Besides, Greg was not the subject of conversation right now, Constance was. Tammy saw the way Greg and Constance were looking at her. Like they were looking at a cornered panther, not quite sure what the unpredictable cat was about to do. If only they both knew how close she was to bursting into tears for the first time in such a long time. She couldn't remember the last time she had shed a tear.

"Honey," Constance tried to reason with Tammy, leaning forward and holding out her hand across the desk for Tammy to take it.

"Let's deal with you first, shall we?" Tammy ignored Constance's offering of peace. Instead, she rested her elbows on the sides of the chair, steepling her fingers. "What is going on with you?"

"I don't know what you mean?" Constance said, sitting back, retracting her hand.

"Oh, come one," Tammy hissed, her eyes hooded. "You've been skulking around here listening in on all the conversation you can since I arrived home. Not to mention all the times I've caught you snooping in mine and Greg's rooms."

"That's a harsh accusation!" Greg immediately defended Constance.

"If you knew what was good for you, you'd butt out of this, or you can get out until I'm ready to deal with you!" Tammy told him harshly.

Tammy saw the anger instantly spark in his eyes at being talked to like he was a servant. But Tammy didn't care. She was beyond caring about liars and manipulators.

"Tammy, you can't speak to people like that," Constance said indignantly. "What has become of you, young lady?"

"I believe that was my question directed at you," Tammy pointed out. "I have places to be, Constance, and I'm growing tired of all the skullduggery going on around here. I've had enough of it all." She tapped her index fingers together. "So, either start talking, or there's the door. I'll get Ashley, who is now my new lawyer, to finalize things here at the ranch for you."

Constance's face once again paled, and she glanced at Greg.

There was a look of both shame and guilt in her eyes, sending alarm bells ringing in Tammy's head.

"Constance?" Greg's brows furrowed as he looked at Constance and Tammy knew he'd seen the look as well. "What's wrong?" He leaned forward and soothingly touched her upper arm.

"I..." Constance broke eye contact and looked down at the apron she was fidgeting with.

Images of that day Tammy arrived flashed through her mind. Constance had looked more worried and guilty than hurt or scared by what had happened. When they'd gotten home, she'd kept pressing for information about Pete and what he'd told the police. Tammy's eyes widened for a split second as the truth suddenly dawned on her. She leaned forward on the desk, resting on her elbows, and clasping her hands in front of her.

"You were involved in what happened on the ranch the day I arrived home!" It wasn't a question but a statement that spilled from Tammy's lips, leaving her feeling cold in its wake.

Greg's head shot around to look at Tammy with a look of shocked surprise. Their eyes locked for a few seconds and Tammy watched the emotion run through his eyes before he broke their eye contact and turned towards Constance.

Greg's voice was hoarse, "That couldn't possibly be true. Please tell Tammy that's not true." His eyes bore into Constance's bowed head and Tammy knew the precise moment he realized it was. "I left my baby girl in your care. I trusted her with you."

"I'm so sorry," Constance sniffed, tears of guilt, shame, and remorse dripping down her cheeks. "I didn't know they were going to take Maggie. When they told me what they were going to do I tried to hide her. I showed her how to use the radio..."

"Stop!" Greg snapped. "Don't say another word." He warned her and pulling out his phone he dialed a number. "Sheriff Haynes, please?"

Tammy frowned at Greg, wondering why he was calling

Sheriff Haynes and not his nephew who was the Lewistown police captain.

"I'm in terrible trouble, aren't I?" Constance looked up at Tammy, who offered her a tissue from the box on the desk.

"That depends on how deeply you're involved with all this and how willing you are to cooperate with law enforcement," Tammy told her. "You are, however, going to need a lawyer." She didn't quite know what to feel about Constance's confession. "Might I suggest Uncle Robert?"

"I could never afford Robert," Constant said through her tears.

"I'm sure he'll work out a plan," Tammy told her.

Tammy knew that there must be some underlying reason why Constance would've played a part in the theft of Double A livestock, but she also knew that Constance had meant it when she'd said she didn't know they would take Maggie. She'd never let anyone harm a child. That is why Tammy took out her phone and once again dialed Robert.

"I knew when you calmed down, you'd come around," Robert answered the phone cheerily. "I think it was Brian's way of ..."

"There's been a development," Tammy cut him off. She was in no mood for small talk.

"Tammy, you didn't kill anyone did you?" Robert's voice went from jovial to serious in two seconds flat.

"I admit that a few minutes ago I could've," Tammy admitted. "But this is not about me. I still want my affairs handed over by Monday. This is about Constance. She needs a lawyer."

There was silence on the other end of the line for a few seconds, "What is going on Tammy?"

"I'm not sure, and I think it's something you best discuss with your client," Tammy told him. "I'll cover the costs as part of her retirement package."

Before Robert could say anything else, she handed the phone to Constance.

"I'm no lawyer," Tammy told her as Constance took her

phone. "But the less you say to us right now the better it will be for you. I'm sure your lawyer will tell you the same."

"I'm going to have to ask for your cell phone and that you wait here in the office for the Sheriff to arrive," Greg's voice was filled with suppressed anger and his eyes blazed as he looked at Constance.

"It's in my room," Constance said softly. "Please, can you take the girls out before the Sheriff arrives?" Her tear-soaked eyes implored Tammy.

"I have to get to Mountain Rise now anyway," Tammy told her. "The girls are both coming with me."

Tammy looked at Greg who nodded. "I'm riding over anyway."

Tammy stood up and walked around the desk. She stopped next to the chair where Constance was sitting and looked at the floor next to her.

"Why did you do whatever it is you did?" Tammy said softly.

"I fell in love," Constance's voice was a whisper, and her head was once again bowed.

"With Pete?" Tammy asked her, not taking her eyes off the spot on the floor.

"Yes," Constance confirmed. "He and a lot of the other ranch hands are fed up with being kept in the dark about the secret sale of the land."

That got both Tammy and Greg's attention.

"Constance, don't say another word!" Robert's voice echoed through the receiver.

"Oh!" Constance looked at the phone startled. "I forgot I still had Robert on the line."

"That's okay," Tammy told her. "It's best he hears what you tell us anyway."

"Put me on speaker," Robert shouted through the phone.

Tammy helped Constance do that.

"Constance is now legally represented by me," Robert's voice was no longer light but it had turned into his courtroom tone.

"Constance, from here on out you speak to no one, not even the police, or sheriff's department without me present."

"What about Tammy and Greg?" Constance's voice wobbled from the tears she'd shed.

"Especially not Tammy and Greg," Robert advised. "My wife is booking tickets as we speak, and we shall be there within... Can't you get Bill to fly us there? There's a landing strip on Four Lakes, so I'll contact the Becketts. Sorry, we'll be there within four to five hours."

"Okay," Constance agreed.

"Tammy and Greg," Robert addressed them. "I know you're both angry right now. But I would very much like you to confirm that Constance is not taken to the local police department."

"I've already arranged for her to be taken in by the Sheriff's department," Greg told him.

"Good," Robert said. "We'll be there in a couple of hours. I know this is not ideal, given how disillusioned you are with me right now, Tammy, but we'll be staying with you."

"Who is we?" Tammy asked.

"Why, your Aunt Molly, and I," Robert informed her. "She's been wanting to get back to Montana for a while now."

"That's just peachy," Tammy said. "I have to go." She looked at Greg. "I'll take the girls and the dogs if you're finished up here?"

Greg said nothing. He only nodded.

Chapter Ten
JOINING FORCES - PART ONE

Tammy didn't say another word when she left the study. She did feel the slightest twinge of guilt for leaving Constance alone with an angry Greg. She did want to know what Constance knew and what she'd meant about the secret sale of the land. But Tammy still had too much anger simmering inside her and she needed to get out of here. She walked up the stairs and found Amy coloring with the two girls in Brynn's room. Three bassets lay scattered across the floor, snoozing in the warm sun streaming into the bright room.

"Come on, all of you," Tammy sail, putting on a bright smile. "We'd better get going or we'll miss out on all the fun."

In all the excitement of going to the barbeque, the two girls and Amy didn't even ask about Constance or Greg, much to Tammy's relief. She'd often laugh when her sister-in-law Lynn would tell her that 'the one thing about parenting is you learn the ability to tell white lies.' Tammy had only been a parent for six months, and she really hadn't mastered that skill yet. She was still mastering saying no candy before dinner or bed. Talking about Constance wouldn't be a simple white lie either, but she knew she also needed to protect two innocent young girls. Brynn and Maggie were already freaked out about what had happened. She didn't want them to know that one of the biggest traitors of all was living right under the same roof as them.

As Tammy pulled out of the drive, she couldn't wait for that evening when Jude would arrive. It wasn't only the two younger girls that would feel safer with him there. Now that she didn't know who to trust anymore, Tammy also needed someone around she could feel safe with.

She didn't like talking business during a fun outing, but she did need to warn Ashley that she'd changed lawyers, and she why did it. Tammy's heart felt like it had been trampled on yet again, once the anger had completely bubbled away.

Tammy had a feeling of déjà vu as she pulled up to the Mountain Rise ranch house, seeing police vehicles and ambulances parked outside. Tammy switched off the engine, watching the paramedics rush out of the front door of the house with someone on the gurney.

"What in the world?" Amy breathed. "Why is it that whenever we arrive at a ranch in Montana there are the police and ambulances in attendance?"

"I hear you," Tammy said, distractedly. "I'm beginning to think we should've stayed in Malibu."

"Well, if you go back there, I'm coming with you!" Maggie piped up from the back seat.

"Of course, sweetheart," Tammy turned and smiled at the girls. "We'd never leave you in this mad place."

The girls giggled at Tammy's comical look.

"Wait here, I'll go find out what is happening," Tammy told them, slipping off her seatbelt and climbing out of the car.

Tammy walked to the house as the ambulance pulled away. She watched Maria and West dash out of the house and climb into her pickup truck. Tammy walked into the house and saw people gathering up their items and getting ready to leave.

"Tammy!" Chelsea called to her, popping out of the room off the side of the hall. "So sorry about all the commotion."

"What on earth is going on?" Tammy asked Chelsea, wide-eyed. "Was that Brett being taken away in the ambulance?"

"Yes." Chelsea nodded. "Sorry, Zac's calling me. Cat and Ashley are out back starting to clean up."

Tammy walked through the house stepping aside to both greet and say goodbye to faces she recognized from growing up in Lewistown. When she popped out of the kitchen and walked out to the backyard, chairs and lawn tables were lying on the side like a stampede of buffalo had rampaged the garden.

"Tammy," Cat waved her over. "Boy did you miss the action!"

"I seem to have a knack of coming in at the tail end of the storm," Tammy said. "What happened?"

Before Cat could relay the story, a horse thundered toward them that she recognized as one of hers. Her heart did a flip in her chest knowing that it was also the horse that Greg always rode.

"I just saw some men driving a herd of horses towards the mountains," Greg called, sliding off the horse and walking over to them stopping as he saw the debris of tables and chairs. "What happened here?"

"I was just about to tell Tammy," Cat told him. "We were about to start the barbeque when Brett was shot."

"What?" Greg breathed, his face paling. "Is he okay?"

"Liam, Maria's son, said he was going to be fine," Cat assured them. "But while everyone was rushing into the house, another shot was fired. The second one we presume was shot so that everyone's attention would be drawn away from what was actually happening."

"They stole Chelsea's livestock and most of the horses," Ashley popped up next to Cat, breathless from having run back from the stables. "I just went to check to see if anyone was hurt down there."

"Who's left inside?" Greg asked Cat.

"Zac, David, and Ryan, I think," Cat answered him.

"I'll go round them up, the horses I saw must be from here. I thought I recognized a few of them." Greg tipped his hat and politely brushed past the three women standing staring after him.

"They took all her livestock?" Tammy frowned. "How could they have done that?"

"I'm not sure," Cat said, her brows also creasing into a frown. "Now that I think about it, how did we not hear the cattle being taken?" She looked at Ashley who shrugged.

"Where were her cattle?" Tammy asked.

"I take it in one of the fields." Cat turned her head.

"I think we should go ask one of the stable hands," Ashley suggested. "They seemed rather chatty when I went to ask about the horses."

"Lead the way," Tammy said.

"Aunt Tammy?" Brynn's voice stopped her, Cat, and Ashley.

"Hi, honey," Tammy turned to look at her niece, Maggie, and Amy standing in the doorway.

"Good grief," Amy breathed.

"Can you look after the girls for a bit?" Tammy asked. "I'm sure they are hungry, and I saw a pile of food in the kitchen." She turned to look at Cat. "Do you think Chelsea would mind if they each had a plate?"

"Of course not," Cat said. "Heaven knows there's a mountain of it."

Amy nodded and pulled the girls back into the kitchen. Tammy, Cat, and Ashley walked to the stables as Zac, Greg, David, and Billy rushed out of the house.

"Cat, can I take Magenta?" Zac asked her.

"Sure," Cat said, frowning. "Where are the four of you going?"

"To find where those horses Greg saw are being taken," Zac told her. "You take my horse, Billy."

Billy nodded and the men got what was left of the horses that had been in the stables, and once they were done, they took off in the direction Greg had seen the other horses.

"Well, that happened," Ashley said.

"I don't like this!" Chelsea watched the horses disappear in the distance.

"What a day!" Cat shook her head. "When is this going to end?"

"I think it will only end once all of us band together and find out what the heck is going on." Tammy bit her bottom lip thoughtfully. "And why this is happening."

"I'm inclined to agree," Chelsea said. "This has gone on for way too long now."

They went back into the stables, looking for one of the stable hands, but they were all missing.

"I'll speak to Zac when he's back," Chelsea told them. "I don't think it's safe for any of us to go looking for the cattle at this particular time."

"I should get the girls and Amy home. My uncle is coming to visit." Tammy's jaw clenched at the thought of her uncle.

The thought of her uncle brought her to Constance. Tammy still couldn't believe kind, caring Constance would've done such a terrible thing, even though Tammy didn't know what exactly she'd done just yet other than somehow being involved with the kidnapping and theft at Double A.

"Thank you so much for coming, Tammy," Chelsea walked Tammy, Amy, Maggie, Brynn,, and the three bassets who had made friends with Chelsea's dogs, out.

After saying her goodbyes, Tammy drove away from Mountain Rise with a terrible feeling of foreboding hanging over her. She glanced at the clock on the dashboard. A few more hours, and Jude would be at the ranch. He was bringing her horse with him that had been stabled at her uncle's ranch. She was so looking forward to seeing her horse again. Before Tammy had left for England, she'd had a few horses but only kept one after she left. He was a special horse she would breed him soon. Tammy just hadn't found the right mare for him yet.

Tammy couldn't help it, but when she pulled into her drive, she found herself holding her breath right up until she pulled up by the garages. When she looked around and the was nothing but calm, she let out a sigh of relief.

"Let's go and make sure Jude's flat is ready for him," Tammy said, climbing out of the car.

"Is he staying in the flatlet downstairs next to Constance's?" Brynn asked her.

At the mention of Constance's name, Tammy stiffened and swallowed. She knew she was going to have to speak to them about Constance. Tammy hated admitting it, but she needed to get Greg's advice on what they would tell the girls.

"Constance had to go away for a little while, so we're going to have to pick up some of her chores," Tammy told them. It wasn't a lie. "The first task is to make sure Jude's rooms are ready for him."

"We also need to make sure your horse's stable is ready for him, Aunt Tammy," Brynn said excitedly.

Brynn had fallen in love with Tammy's horse when she'd taken her riding, and Tammy knew her horse had felt the same way about Brynn. She'd never seen her stallion be so gentle with anyone in his entire life. The horse was a demon that loved to give everyone who wasn't Tammy a hard time.

Brynn had surprised Tammy with both her horse handling skills and horsemanship. She had absolutely no fear when it came to horses and was totally horse mad. Her uncle Robert had gone as far as to say that Brynn reminded him of her at that age. It wasn't until that moment that Tammy realized just how much fear she must've driven into her parents' and brother's heart with her horse antics.

"Aunt Tammy?" Maggie said softly, breaking into Tammy's thoughts. "Your phone's ringing."

"Oh, thank you, love." Tammy smiled, pulling her phone out of her jacket pocket. It was her uncle. "Can you take the girls in and give Jude's flat a once over? I have to take this."

Amy nodded and then ushered the girls and three bassets into the house.

"Hello," Tammy's voice was cold and business-like.

"We'll be there in two hours," Robert told her. "Is Greg with you?"

"No, he is not," Tammy said, her voice now clipped. "But whatever you need to say to him, you can say to me. We are, after all, co-owners of *my* family home and legacy now."

"Tammy." Robert sighed. "I needed to ask him where they are holding Constance."

"As the sheriff personally came and took her away, I would think at the sheriff's office," Tammy told him.

"Oh, that would explain why no one at the police station could find her," Robert said.

"I specifically heard Greg say to you the Sheriff was on his way," Tammy pointed out.

"A lot was going on around me, Tammy," Robert said. "Your aunt wants to have a word with you."

"Hello, sweetheart," Molly, Robert's wife, came on the line. "Now, I know you're cross with your uncle, but I hope that feeling is not directed towards me as well?"

"Only if you knew what he was hiding, Aunt Molly," Tammy said honestly.

"I can assure you that I most certainly did not," Molly said indignantly. "When I asked why you'd fired him and he told me, make no mistake, I told him exactly what all kinds of a fool he'd been."

Tammy grinned. She did not doubt that Aunt Molly would have given Robert quite a tongue lashing. Tammy knew she hated lies, secrets, and deceit more than anyone.

"Well, then I'm not mad at you, Aunt Molly." Tammy glanced around the ranch. It was rather quiet, but, then again, there had just been an upset at Mountain Rise, so everyone must be there. "I will get one of the guest rooms ready for you, Aunt Molly, although we'll have to have take-out tonight."

"Nonsense," Aunt Molly said. "We're not getting in that late. I will cook."

"No, I can't expect you to do that after such a long trip," Tammy said. "There are too many of us to cook for."

"Child, I have a rather larger family, if you remember?" Molly laughed.

"I'll cook, Aunt Molly." Tammy sighed.

"You most certainly will not!" Molly sounded almost insulted. "Heavens, we both know that you, my love, are not the best cook, and I'm sorry, but I cannot put myself through that again."

Tammy knew she should have been insulted, but she couldn't be. She agreed with her aunt. Tammy was a terrible cook, and the few times she'd tried to host a dinner party where she did the cooking, she'd nearly poisoned her guests. She burst out laughing, remembering the looks on the faces of all those that attempted to eat her cooking.

"Now that's the sound I've missed for a long, long time." Molly's voice was soft. "Anyway, I need to balance my way to the girl's room in this tiny excuse of a plane."

"Have a safe flight, Aunt Molly, and I'll see you soon." Tammy hung up once her aunt said her goodbyes.

Aunt Molly always knew how to soothe Tammy's ruffled feathers and bruised heart. Tammy gave one more glance around the ranch, shaking off the weird feeling that she was being watched. It was more likely she was being paranoid after everything that had happened. She locked her car and walked into the house, closing and locking the door behind her – something they hardly ever did except at night. Tammy shuddered, taking off her jacket and hat to hang on the stand next to the door.

She followed the sound of giggling, barking, and music to the flat next to the one Constance had lived in for over forty sixty years. Sadness gripped her heart when she stared at the closed door. It was usually always slightly ajar in case anyone needed her. Tammy swallowed the lump in her throat, turning to go to Jude's apartment. When this house was built in the seventeen hundreds, this part of the house contained servant quarters. There were three one-bedroom flats, five bedrooms, and two bathrooms. Each flat obviously had its own bathroom while the bedrooms shared the two others.

"I hear there's a party going on in here?" Tammy smiled, watching Maggie, Brynn, and Amy dancing as they made sure the flatlet was ready for Jude.

"Come dance with us, Aunt Tammy," Brynn laughed, running to her, and grabbing her hands, pulling her into the room.

Tammy laughed and let herself be lured into a dance while she inspected the place.

"Can I have the cleaning spray?" Tammy asked Ashely when she saw some dust on the bookshelf in the small living area near the front of the flat.

"Sure. Here, catch." Amy threw the bottle of liquid at Tammy.

It flew right for her head, and just before it hit her between the eyes, a large hand flashed in front of her nose and caught the bottle.

"Nice catch," Amy said to the catcher, her cheeks going red. "I'm so sorry, Tam."

Tammy's head flew around to see Greg standing so close next to her she could feel the warmth emanating from his body. Her heart did a few jumps, and something knotted in her stomach.

"I can't compliment you on your throwing, though." Greg handed Tammy the bottle. "I believe this is for you?"

"Thank you," Tammy managed to squeak still a little shaken by a bottle being hurled at her head and from being so close to Greg.

Tammy took a step away from him, drawing his attention to her. His green and gold eyes looked at her. He raised his eyebrow as a small knowing smile curved the one side of his mouth.

The arrogant jerk! Tammy fumed, before turning her back on him to quickly spray down the bookshelf.

"Who is all this for?" Greg asked. "Are you putting your uncle and aunt down here?"

"Are Uncle Robert and Aunt Molly coming here?" Brynn's eyes widened with excitement when she heard her uncle and aunt's names. Robert and Molly were their only living relations in that generation.

"Yes, they are," Tammy was grateful for the interruption. She turned and smiled at Brynn. "That's why, when we're done here, we need to go and fix up the guest room next to Greg's room for them."

"Sure," Maggie and Brynn said together before running from the room.

Brynn stopped and glanced back into it, "The blue room or the rose room?"

"Aunt Molly has always loved the rose room," Tammy told them and shuddered. "Although I don't know how anyone could possibly sleep in a room with that rose wallpaper."

"I think it's lovely, Aunt Tammy," Maggie said before she, and Brynn, ran off.

"I'd better go and keep an eye on them," Amy said, whistling for the bassets who loped after her out of the flatlet.

Suddenly, Tammy and Greg were alone, and an awkward silence descended over the room. Tammy wished that Maggie had left her music in the room. Not knowing what to do, she glanced at her watch.

"I'd better go and see that there are supplies for Aunt Molly to cook dinner with," Tammy said, turning to leave.

But before she could walk away, Greg's hand shot out and grabbed her arm, stopping her.

"We need to talk," Greg's voice was soft and full of meaning.

"Can this wait until tomorrow maybe?" Tammy's skin burned at his touch, and her pulse had instantly become erratic.

Inwardly, Tammy seethed at her traitorous body and heart. There was no way she would fall for this man again. Once, he had nearly destroyed her, and she was still sifting through the debris of enough recent emotional devastation in her life. Tammy was not ready to face any more.

"No, we need to talk now," Greg insisted.

Tammy's eyes met his, and she sucked in her breath when she saw the torment and guilt in their depth. She was about to yank her arm away and tell him he'd have to wait until tomorrow until she saw that pain in his eyes.

"Fine," Tammy relented. "Can you give me an hour to get the

room ready and my horse settled?" She glanced at her watch. "He should be arriving any minute now."

"He?" Greg gave her a small smile. "You have another stallion?"

"Yes, my horse is a he," Tammy said stupidly and felt her cheeks heat. *Good grief, get a grip, you silly woman, you're not eighteen.* "You should come meet him. I think you'll like him."

"I will come and help get him settled," Greg said. "I've always loved watching you work with horses." His voice dropped, and a different emotion flashed in his but was gone too quickly for her to decipher.

Greg still had not let go of her arm, and Tammy had not stepped out of his grip. They stood staring at each other for a few seconds, and Tammy could feel that old familiar pull towards him. She swallowed and licked her lips, noting his eyes dropping to them. Tammy felt her pulse quicken even more under his green and gold gaze.

"Aunt Tammy!" Brynn's excited voice shouted down the hallway. "They're here!"

The door banged open. Greg dropped his hand, and Tammy turned to smile at her niece while forcing her shaking legs to walk normally as she followed Brynn to the back door.

"Who's here?" Tammy asked her.

"Jude and Stormy," Brynn said excitedly, rushing outside as a pickup with a horse trailer pulled into the yard with Maggie and Amy hot on her heels.

"Wait up, you." Tammy laughed, rushing after out the door. She saw Maggie, who was standing next to Brynn, looking just as excited to meet her horse.

Tammy didn't have to turn around to know that Greg had followed them. She could hear the soft fall of his feet and feel his eyes on her back.

"JP!" Brynn squealed in delight, dashing towards Jude as he climbed out of the vehicle.

"Hey, Brynn." Jude laughed.

Jude bent down, opened his arms, caught her, spun her

around, and tossed her in the air like she weighed no more than a baseball. Tammy held her breath until he caught her like he always did when they did this.

"Does he always do that?" Greg startled her, coming up to stand next to her.

"Pretty much," Amy answered for Tammy, coming up next to them. "Every time he does it, I bet that Tammy will punch him."

"Well, I'm glad I'm not the only one then," Greg said.

"Don't worry. He's only dropped her four..." Amy made a face while she calculated. "Maybe eight times."

"What?!" Greg's eyes blazed as they shot to Amy, who started to laugh.

"Relax," Amy said, still laughing. "I'm joking. Jude is great with Brynn, and I wouldn't trust anyone else with her. Trust me, we're all safer with him here, and maybe Maggie will start to settle down again as well."

"Hi," Jude had been introduced to Maggie and walked up to them, drawing a smile from Tammy.

Jude had a girl hanging from each muscular arm, which he held out at shoulder height next to him. Three bassets flopped around his feet as he came up to them as if it was totally normal.

"I see you know how two handle monkeys hanging from your arms." Tammy grinned.

"I bet Jude couldn't carry us like this," Brynn told her, looking like she was about to be roasted over an open fire.

"Man, you have the longest arms I've ever seen," Amy whistled beneath her breath.

"Jude," Greg greeted him. "It's been a long time. How are you?"

"Greg!" Jude looked surprised to see him. "I didn't know you were on detail here." He looked from one arm to the next. "I'd shake hands, but I made a bet with these two that I could hold them like this for longer than fifteen minutes."

"Ah!" Greg's lips twitched at the sight.

Jude was still in top-notch shape for a man of fifty-four. He was also still very handsome, with a few grey hairs scattered in his thick blond hair. He was extremely tall. Jude topped Greg's six-foot-three by two inches.

"How long do you have to go?" Amy asked.

"Another six minutes," Jude smiled at Amy.

"So, what do they win if you lose the bet?" Amy gave Jude a sideways glance, and Tammy didn't like the look in her eyes. She was up to something.

"Jude's going to treat us to a triple scoop with all the toppings at Aunt Holly's coffee shop." Brynn's looked at Amy upside down.

"Can I get in on that bet?" Amy tilted her head sideways to look at Brynn.

"Of course," Maggie shouted from the other arm.

"Cool." Amy nodded. She grinned and turned to Tammy with an innocent look on her face. "I taught Derby a new trick."

"What are you up to?" Tammy's eyes narrowed as she watched Amy. She knew that look, and it usually meant someone was about to be pranked.

"Oh, nothing, but Derby's been dying to show off his new trick." Amy turned to Jude with an evil smile curving her lips.

"Amy..." Jude warned her, not liking the look in her eyes either.

"You're going to love this!" Amy looked at Derby. "Derby!"

The dog instantly stood to attention and looked at Amy.

"Hidden treat!" Amy pointed to Jude's jeans pocket.

Derby's head shot around to look at Jude's pocket. He gave a small gruff, then pounced on Jude's leg knocking him off balance with his weight.

Jude wobbled and tried to steady himself while Maggie and Brynn started to giggle. The other two bassets decided to get in on the fun game. Soon Jude landed on the ground, desperately trying to keep the girls from harm. Two laughing girls and three basset hounds tumbled on top of him in a heap in the dirt.

"So," Amy leaned down, pulling dogs and kids off Jude. "When are we going for these ice creams?" She smiled sweetly down at him, ignoring the daggers shooting at her from his eyes.

"Are you two and the dogs alright?" Jude asked, jumping to his feet, and checking to ensure no person or animal was hurt.

The girls both nodded between giggles, and the bassets wanted to play more they jumped about barking excitedly.

"That's cheating!" Jude glared at Amy.

"Is it, though?" Amy scrunched up her face. "You just said you made a bet that you could hold the girls like that for fifteen minutes." She shook her head. "You never stipulated anything else. But then you clearly couldn't hold them like that. Aren't you taught to focus or something in the army or bodyguard school?"

"You're lucky I had the training I had," Jude told her, shaking his head.

"Okay, that's enough!" Tammy decided it was time to step in and save poor Jude. "I'm sure Jude is exhausted after his long drive here."

"I'm good, really," Jude assured Tammy, turning away from the grinning Amy. "But I do know someone who needs to get out for a bit."

Jude turned and started walking towards the horsebox.

"Amy, that wasn't nice," Tammy hissed as she walked past her.

"All's fair in love and ice cream." Amy shrugged, grinning. "You have to admit it was funny, though."

"It was!" Greg agreed with Amy, fist-bumping her as he walked with them to the horsebox.

"Oh, my word, Aunt Amy, he's beautiful!" Maggie's voice was filled with Awe when she and Brynn were the first to get to the horsebox. "I don't think I've ever seen anything as beautiful as him."

Chapter Eleven
JOINING FORCES - PART TWO

Greg couldn't believe what a terrible day it had been. He needed to come home and talk to Tammy before her uncle and aunt arrived. Greg didn't want any more animosity between them than there already was. That is why he needed to clear up this mess with Brian's estate. Even though he was irritated by the man's arrival time, Greg was pleased that Jude Pike was here. He hadn't realized Jude was the security detail Tammy had hired to protect Brynn and Amy in Malibu.

Brynn referred to him as JP, and Greg hadn't put it together. He may have if his mind wasn't so full of everything happening around them right now. The complications just seemed to keep growing and growing. Today, one of his deepest fears and suspicions had been proven true. Greg was now more convinced than ever that he knew why all this was happening to the ranches. But he still had to figure out the who because there seemed to be more than one of those.

Greg heard his daughter's delight when she laid eyes on Tammy's horse, piquing his interest. He walked around the back of the trailer as Jude skillfully guided a big, pure black thoroughbred with two white streaks in his black tail and mane out of the box. The horse didn't seem at all fussed by the kids or the dogs as they walked alongside it.

"Well, he's a lot calmer than the last thoroughbred stallion I remember you owned," Greg said to Tammy softly.

"Give him a minute," Tammy warned. "He's always a little placid when he first gets out of the box."

"Does that mean I should pull my daughter and Brynn out of his way?" Greg kept an eye on the breathtakingly beautiful horse.

The animal's gleaming black coat glinted in the sunlight. He had a lightning bolt white patch down the center of his face. The white streaks in his mane and tail made him unique.

"No. Strangely enough, he's really good with children," Tammy told him. "It's grown men he doesn't like."

"Ah, typical stallion not liking any other male competition," Greg gave a soft laugh. "He seems to like Jude just fine."

"He's known Jude for a few months now," Tammy said. "Trust me, it took a good while before Jude could even get close to him."

"How did he get close to him then?" Greg's eyes collided with Tammy's, and, suddenly, his question seemed to have a completely different meaning than what he intended.

"Is that okay, Aunt Tammy?" Brynn's voice hit him like a slap in the face, pulling him out of a trance.

"Sorry?" Tammy's eyes pulled away from his making him feel like something had been taken from him.

"Can we go with JP to let Stormy run in the back paddock?" Brynn repeated, her young brow creased in a frown as she gave Tammy a peculiar look.

Tammy looked at Greg for confirmation, which shocked Greg so much that he just nodded.

"Jude, please don't let them out of your sight!" Greg barked. "Let me know right away if there's even a hint of trouble."

Jude tapped his jacket pocket and pulled out a small box. He walked over to Greg and opened it.

"Take one." Jude picked up his earpiece from inside the box while offering the other to Greg. "I brought these because of all the trouble at the ranches. I was going to get some more security, if necessary, although I believe Wallace Black is in these parts with some men."

"Thank you." Greg took the other one and popped it in his ear, taking the box Jude held out. "Yes, he is." He nodded, "When you settled in, I'll give Wallace a call and get him over here. He is between Cupids Bow Ranch and Big Valley Ranch most of the time."

"Good, I'd prefer not to have to go over there and keep an eye out here," Jude said. "Especially after what happened to your daughter. I was really sorry to hear about that."

"Thanks, Jude," Greg told him. "I'm glad you're here."

Jude nodded and walked a little way away before testing the earpiece communication. "Can you hear me?"

"Yes," Greg confirmed.

"Okay, James Bond," Tammy said to Jude. "The kids are rolling their eyes at you more impatiently than Storm is right now."

"Do I need to have Amy with us?" Jude grumbled.

"Don't let her bully you," Tammy laughed, leaning close to Greg's ear to speak to Jude as he walked towards the impatient kids. "She'll help you with Storm if he gets antsy. You know he likes her."

"I always thought your horse had trouble judging human nature," Jude grumbled, making Tammy laugh.

Greg cleared his throat and took a deep silent breath to calm his rising pulse and steady the erratic heart rate her closeness was causing him. Once again, when Tammy took a few steps away from him to put some space between them, he felt as if something had been ripped from him.

"Storm?" Greg said, looking at Tammy and referencing her horse's name wanting to keep the conversation between them light as he was enjoying how relaxed she seemed.

"Yes, he's the grandson of Storm Front," Tammy shocked him by saying.

"So, you did keep Storm Front?" Greg looked at her, amazed.

Tammy had told him she had sold the horse because she

hadn't wanted any reminders of him in her life. Greg didn't know why he felt a spark of pleasure knowing she'd kept the horse that had ultimately brought them together. He also felt foolish that he'd spent years keeping an eye out for the blasted horse when Tammy had him in LA.

"I did," was all Tammy said. "Do you want to go have our meeting now?"

Greg gave an inward sigh. The aloofness was back in Tammy's eyes as she looked at him and her voice was no longer warm but business-like. Greg now knew what it must feel like to be one of Tammy's clients as he nodded and then followed her into the house. They walked into the study, and Tammy waited for him to enter before closing the door. She walked around the desk and sat in the chair Greg was used to seeing her brother, Brian, in. His heart gave a painful thud as he thought of his best friend. Brian and his young wife's lives had been taken too soon. Greg knew it was highly unlikely, but he couldn't help but feel Brian's death wasn't an accident.

Greg pulled out a chair in front of Tammy, the same chair he'd sat in earlier when they'd interrogated Constance. He gave himself a mental shake. Greg still couldn't believe that Constance had betrayed them like she had. He'd known Constance since he was four years old. She'd been there when Brynn's mother had gone into labor, there when he'd come to stay with Brian when his ex-wife had left them, and he had trusted her with his kids.

"Greg?" Tammy's soft voice brought him back from his reverie. He glanced up at her and, for a few moments, saw compassion shining in her deep blue eyes like she knew what he was thinking. "Are you okay?"

Greg's breath had caught in his throat at the look. He couldn't trust his voice, so he nodded.

"You want to talk to me?" The look of compassion was gone, replaced by a cool neutral look as Tammy sat back in her chair.

"I wanted to explain what Brian did and why he did it," Greg told her.

Tammy's expression didn't change. She simply nodded and watched him intently.

"About four months before the avalanche, Brian came to me and needed to talk to me." Greg swallowed. It was still hard for him to talk about Brian, who was more like a brother to him than just a friend.

"Robert did tell me that Brian was hounding him to make sure his affairs were in order," Tammy told Greg. "Robert and I were worried that he may have gotten some bad health news. But when I spoke to Brian, he assured me he was perfectly healthy but hadn't updated his will or checked on all his insurance policies in a good five years." Her eyes narrowed, and she bit her bottom lip thoughtfully. "But I'm guessing there was more to it than that?"

"Yes." Greg nodded. "Brian was convinced that someone was trying to harm him."

"What?" Tammy's brows drew together.

"I don't know if he told Robert this," Greg said. "But there'd been some freak accidents around the ranch."

"Freak accidents?" Tammy's brows tightened even more.

"Yes, his horse's saddle had been tampered with, and he nearly had a bad accident." Greg knew by the shock in Tammy's eyes that she hadn't known about the incidents. "Then there was the tractor coming for him, and the last straw was the car accident."

"Excuse me?" Tammy's brows shot up in shock, and her face paled. "What car accident? Why wouldn't Brian tell me something like that?"

"Because he didn't even tell his wife," Greg told her softly. "I'm not sure if Lynn knew about any of the accidents. They seemed to all be targeted specifically at him."

"Where is his pickup truck?" Tammy looked at him questioningly. "I've been meaning to ask since I arrived, but things have been so busy and action-packed around here."

"It's parked in my garage at the store in Lewistown." Greg's voice dropped. "I got my son to collect it when it was ready and park it there as I..." His voice wobbled, and he swallowed, pushing down the emotion that tried to break free.

"I understand," Tammy's voice was hoarse, and when he looked at her, he saw his emotions regarding Brian mirrored in her eyes. "I haven't been in his and Lynn's room. I know he took over our parent's bedroom when he married Lynn. I couldn't go in there after my dad died, and I still can't go in there now."

"Yeah, Constance kept telling me that I had to go in there and clean it out," Greg told her. "But I couldn't. When she said she'd do it, I freaked out at her, locked the room, and hid the key."

His eyes had dropped to look at the desk where his finger was tapping on the surface, but they shot up when they heard Tammy's soft laugh. Their eyes met and held. Greg saw the emotions swirling in their heady blue depth. In those few moments, as they were locked in each other's gazes, their hearts joined in mourning a lost loved one. Greg had a strong compulsion to reach over and touch her. He wanted to pull Tammy to him, wrap his arms around her to let each of them draw comfort from the other; the comfort they so needed from not having been able to mourn their brother and his wife properly.

Greg knew from that look that, like him, Tammy had to push aside the temptation to crumple to her knees and let the heart-wrenching pain and despair of loss out. They were both the apex members of their families, households, and businesses. People turned to them for their support, their strength, and guidance. Greg and Tammy didn't have the luxury of breaking. They had to push on through whatever storm blew their way, protecting those that relied on them to make sure they were okay and then being there after the storm to make sure all the pieces were put back together.

"Thank you for that," Tammy's voice was suspiciously hoarse, and her eyes sparkled with unshed tears, but she managed to gather herself quickly. "Especially after what Constance has done. I would've hated her going through my brother or Lynn's things."

"Tammy, we still don't know why Constance did what she did." Greg sat back in his chair and moved his hands to the armrests. "I think we both need to hear her out when Robert is here."

"Do you think Robert is going to let us near her?" Tammy's eyes narrowed, and Greg saw the anger flash in them. "We can discuss Constance later." She changed the subject. "Finish what you wanted to tell me about Brian."

"Right!" Greg snapped back to the cold reality where Tammy held him a good few arm lengths at bay and assessed him with cool, mistrusting eyes while he harbored his own ill feelings towards her.

"Tell me about Brian's accident." Tammy looked at him expectantly.

"He wouldn't tell me much about it. I had to pry the information from my nephew."

Greg shook his head, remembering how Brain had shut down about the accident. All he said was the less Greg knew about anything the better it would be for Greg.

"Brian wouldn't tell me much about it. What I know I got from my nephew, Parker," Greg told her honestly. "That accident happened a few days before the skiing trip."

"But you feel there were a lot more incidences than Brian let on, don't you?" Tammy's eyes scrutinized him.

"I do," Greg admitted. "After the avalanche, the ranch hands were all in shock, and a few of them started to open up to me. I know that Brian was trapped in the store when a mysterious fire broke out in it. I know about Brian being trapped in the indoor arena at Cupids Bow when they were preparing for the spring show. One of the rodeo bulls was set free in it."

"WHAT?" Tammy choked, her face had paled, and her blue eyes were wide with shock. "All that happened, and Brian didn't say a word to me or you?" Her wide-eyed look changed to narrowed-eyed contemplation. "Do you think Lynn knew at least?"

"I'm not sure," Greg told Tammy honestly. "Brian didn't want to discuss the accidents. All he said was the less I knew about anything the better, as it had already taken too many lives." He frowned. "The most recent one had been the death of Todd Beckett, Ryan's older brother."

"I thought Todd had a heart attack?" Tammy said, looking confused.

"No." Greg frowned at Tammy. It was his turn to look confused. "Who told you that?"

"Brian," Tammy said.

"Todd was killed in a hit and run accident in Lewistown eighteen months ago," Greg told her and saw the shock hit Tammy. "I'm sorry!"

"I..." Tammy swallowed, and Greg could see her struggling. "Are you sure?"

"I'm afraid so." Greg felt awful having to tell her the truth about Todd's death. "I know you were close when you were younger."

Greg couldn't stop that instant hot flash of jealousy that shot through his stomach like acid when he thought of Todd's relationship with Tammy. Todd was part of Greg's group of friends as they were all the same age and went to school together. Todd also had a giant crush on Tammy, even though he always insisted that they were just friends. Tammy had always felt more comfortable with Todd than with Brian's friends. Well, Todd and West when he was around. But Tammy and Todd were close. Greg had been really surprised when he'd found out that Todd was marrying Alicia Hill. A few nights before the wedding, Todd had confessed to having been in love with Alicia all through high school, but Greg hadn't believed a word because he'd seen how Todd had looked at Tammy.

"Greg, I'm sorry about your friend," Tammy's voice once again drew him out of his memories. "I know you and Todd were close."

"Yes, it was a horrible shock," Greg admitted. "Todd had just left the auction house, and I was walking back to the pens when I heard screaming, and the screeching of wheels." He shuddered and pinched the bridge of his now. "It was dreadful. The driver never stopped, he just carried on driving. The car disappeared. The street cameras couldn't pick up anything either. There were no plates on the car, no clear shots of the driver, and the witnesses were more focused on Todd than the car."

"Oh, no," Tammy's voice was once again hoarse, and her eyes misted over. "He didn't deserve that. I know he was still not over Alicia's death a few years before."

"Gwen, Ryan, his son Travis, and Avery were devastated," Greg told her. "Ryan is still trying to hunt down who the driver was."

"I can imagine. Ryan is like that. He won't stop either." Tammy shook her head. Her eyes were filled with sorrow. A quiet fell over them, which she broke a few seconds later, "What is going on around here, Greg?" Her eyes clouded with worry. "What has happened to our once peaceful and carefree home?"

"I..." Before Greg could answer, Tammy's phone rang.

"Hello, Robert!" Tammy's voice immediately became cool and clipped again.

He watched her nod. "Fine, I'll send Jude to pick you up."

"Have they landed?" Greg asked, feeling disappointed his time alone with Tammy was coming to a quick end.

"In forty minutes, give or take a few minutes," Tammy told. "Can you ask Jude to take my car and go fetch them, please? I'm okay for him to take Brynn if you're okay for him to take Maggie with?"

Greg nodded and contacted Jude.

"I told him to take my SUV because Amy wants to go along for a drive," Greg told her. "It has more seats."

"Ah, that's your SUV in the garage?" Tammy asked him.

"It is," Greg confirmed.

"We still have some time," Tammy leaned back in her seat once again. "Please continue telling me about Brian."

"To cut a long story short, Brian was more than a bit paranoid before the avalanche," Greg told Tammy truthfully. "He wanted to make sure all his affairs were in order. A few days before he, Lynn, and Brynn went away, he pulled me in here to tell me about his will."

"To tell you that he'd given you one quarter of his share of the property, the house, and the cattle!" Tammy guessed.

"Yes," Greg confirmed. "I told him I didn't want that, but he insisted. He said that if anything happened to him, he knew you'd come home to take over. Brian was scared that what was happening to him would then revert to you."

"Sounds like something Brian would do." Tammy sighed and sunk back. "Why didn't he just come out and tell me about all this?" She looked at Greg questioningly. "From what I've heard and now witnessed around here, Brian isn't the only one being targeted."

"No, he isn't," Greg told her honestly. "It seems a whole lot of us are being targeted."

Tammy's eyes shot to his in shocked surprise, "Us?" Her brows lifted as she stared at him.

"Yes," Greg admitted. "My house wasn't an accident." His voice was low as he tried to control that slow, burning anger that started to boil when he thought of his family home. "Termites had weakened a lot of the building's structure. We'd just gotten a handle on infestation after infestation when that storm struck."

"You think someone was trying to destroy your property?" Tammy's eyes widened.

"Yes." Greg nodded. "We had endless vandalism with smashed windows, gates, and doors."

"I'm sorry, Greg," Tammy's eyes were again filled with compassion, but this time he could see a flame of anger flickering behind it. This time, the anger wasn't directed at him but at whoever was terrorizing his family. "You have children as well. How can people be so callous?"

"The fourth time our house was broken into Brian decided enough was enough and moved us here for a few weeks until the house was repaired," Greg explained. "I was so grateful because the trouble had really affected Maggie."

"I can only imagine," Tammy's voice was filled with the emotion shining in her big blue eyes.

"When the house had been fixed, we went home and two weeks later, found our first termite infestations," Greg told her. "As you know, most of our old house is made of wood. They hit all the major structures as if they were trained to do so."

"An army of termites." Tammy shook her head. "I don't understand why they'd pick on you, though." She frowned. "I thought it was only mine and the four ranches surrounding Double A."

"Oh, no," Greg shook his head. "The trouble has been extended to the Cuthberts, the hospital, a few of the older doctors, even some of the older nurses, and even Holly's café."

"Really?" Tammy's expression changed to one of thoughtful contemplation. "I guess there are a lot of people in that group that are friends with the five ranches."

"That's one way to look at it," Greg agreed and was about to say something else when Tammy's eyes widened as something dawned on her.

"You don't think that..." Tammy shook her head and slumped back again. "No, that's too absurd."

"What is?" Greg asked her with a growing feeling that Tammy had come to the same assumption about the avalanche.

"You're going to think I'm mad and probably looking for someone to blame here," Tammy told him. "But what is the avalanche that took my brother's life wasn't a natural one after all?"

"Thank goodness," Greg knew he'd surprised her by saying. "That was the first thought that crossed my mind when I heard about the avalanche."

"Oh?" Tammy looked at him, pleasantly surprised. "But what are the chances of that?"

"If you look at the big picture leading up to that accident, I think the chances seem way bigger," Greg told her. "The thing is, how do we go about finding something like that out?"

"Another question is why did someone want Brian dead so

badly they'd kill, injure, and risk an entire ski resort to do it?" Tammy said.

"Maybe they were looking to take out more people than just Brian?" Greg told her. "It was also a private ski resort that only took so many exclusive guests. I think the only reason Brian got in there was because of..." He swallowed. He really didn't want to bring up more bad memories for Tammy.

"My estranged, now late husband, Martin Guest?" Tammy finished for him. "You can say his name." She gave him a small smile. "I don't wish anyone dead, and it is a shock to know he is gone, but things between us had been over for a long time."

"I wonder if there is a way to get a guest list for that day." Greg looked at Tammy thoughtfully. "Do you think maybe Robert could pull some strings for us?"

"I doubt the resort would talk to Robert," Tammy told him. "But they'd talk to me."

"Oh?" Greg looked at her curiously.

"I know the owners of the resort," Tammy explained to him. "I've often set up ski vacations for some of my clients."

"Right," Greg had nearly forgotten corporate Tammy for a moment, especially now that she was dressed more like a cowgirl than an executive. "Do you think it's worth looking into?"

"I'm inclined to say yes," Tammy said. "I know it's a long shot, but avalanches can be triggered by someone."

"I know," Greg nodded.

"It just seems too much of a coincidence not to look into," Tammy spoke Greg's thoughts. "Especially when you say Brian was having trouble." She frowned, sat back for a minute, then started opening the drawers of his desk.

"What are you looking for?" Greg asked her, craning his neck to see what she was doing.

"Do you remember how Brian liked to jot significant moments in his life down?" Tammy stopped searching and sat back in the chair with a thoughtful look on her face.

"Yes." Greg nodded and realized where she was going with

this conversation. "Do you think he jotted down the incidents?" His eyes widened.

"It's something else worth looking into," Tammy told him.

"Definitely." Greg cocked his head and looked around the office. "What about the safe?"

Tammy and Greg both looked at the picture of one of Tammy's pirate-turned-cowboy ancestors that hung on the wall. Greg smiled to himself, knowing how much she hated that picture. But before they could get to check it out, they heard a car pulling up.

"Oh no," Tammy surprised him by saying. "They're here already."

"What do you want to do?" Greg asked her.

"Keep this door locked," Tammy said, "and don't under any circumstance give anyone else the key to Brian's room either."

"I won't," Greg promised her. "So, does this mean we're teaming up?" He grinned.

"I guess it does," Tammy told him. "Thank you, Greg, for telling me the truth about Brian. I believe that my brother thought he was protecting me, Brynn, and Lynn, by doing what he did. Although I wouldn't have agreed with him if he'd told me about it because of our stormy past, I'm now glad he did."

Greg stared at her in complete shock. He felt the tiny zaps zing all his nerves as she continued.

"This is not a time where I'd like to be alone here," Tammy continued. "Even with Jude. I feel you and I are better here as a united front. He can look after the kids and Amy while we are digging deeper into the matter at hand."

"Agreed," was all Greg managed to say through his shock.

"But let's also agree that we keep this between us. We also agree to complete honesty about our findings and what we are doing," Tammy stipulated. "If we are going to team up we need to put the past behind us and concentrate on the here and now."

"I'm with you on everything, one hundred percent," Greg assured her.

"Great," Tammy stepped around the desk, holding out her

hand. "We will meet early tomorrow morning again. Let's go for a ride so we know we're not overheard."

Greg swallowed at her invitation and hardly realized his large hand had engulfed hers until he felt her warm, soft skin melt into his sending his heart into overdrive. He gave himself a mental shake and gathered what wits he had left.

"Partners?" Greg shook her hand.

"Partners." Tammy agreed. "There are two keys to the study. You take one, and I'll keep the other."

"I'll give you the other key to Brian's room," Greg told her.

They'd just stepped and locked the office door when the front door burst open. Maggie, Brynn, and three excited bassets broke through, followed by a laughing Molly.

"There's my beautiful niece," Molly spotted Tammy walking towards her and threw her arms out to engulf her.

Greg stood back, watching the greeting take place, noticing Robert's jovial greeting of Tammy was received with a stiff icy glare from her. Robert sighed and watched sadly as Tammy turned to walk with Molly, Amy, the kids, and three bassets up the stairs.

"She's never going to forgive me, is she?" Robert sighed as he wandered over to Greg to shake his hand. "How are you holding up under her anger?"

"Oh, we're past that now," Greg smiled at the look of shock on Robert's face. "Jude!" He looked past Robert as Jude staggered in lumbered with luggage.

"Where should I take these?" Jude asked.

"I'll help you," Greg rushed forward to take some of the luggage. "Follow me."

"You wanted to speak to me?" Jude asked, following Greg up the stairs and towards the room Tammy had prepared for her guests.

"Yes," Greg told him. "Let's get these bags to the room first, and we can chat while we get your luggage to your apartment."

"Oh, no." Jude shook his head. "I promised Brynn and

Maggie I wouldn't go to my apartment until they were ready to show me."

"I see." Greg couldn't help but smile. Tammy really couldn't have picked a better bodyguard than Jude Pike, he thought once again. "I see you've been totally taken over by my daughter and Brynn?"

"They're great kids," Jude told him as they walked into the room where Brynn and Maggie were showing Molly around.

"Where do you want these?" Greg asked Molly.

"Greg!" Molly walked up to him.

Her golden blonde hair was neatly coiffed, and she had a big warm smile on her beautiful face that had aged gracefully. Even casually dressed in jeans and a soft cotton shirt, she looked like she was off to a country club lunch.

"Hi, Molly." Greg went in for the obligatory hug.

"You're still as strappingly handsome as ever," Molly grinned with a glint of mischief in her eyes as if she was planning something. "It's a wonder that you haven't been snapped up by some woman by now." She glanced over at Tammy, who was trying to stop one of her bassets from jumping onto the bed.

"I don't know what you're planning, Molly," Greg told her. "But please don't."

"I'm not planning anything," Molly looked at him innocently. "I just worry about your happiness." She looked at Tammy, who was laughing at something Maggie was saying. "Yours and my beautiful niece's."

"I think we're going to be fine," Greg assured Molly. "We just need to get all the trouble that's hit town settled."

"I've heard there's been more." Molly had been distracted from her previous thoughts.

"Unfortunately, Brett Parker was shot," Greg told her. "West sent me a message a little while ago, telling me that he was out of surgery now, and the doctors said he'd be okay."

"No one is ever okay after they've been shot." Molly's brown eyes glinted with anger and worry. "We must send the Parkers a get-well basket."

"Of course," Greg said. "I'll see to that."

"Oh, no, you won't, young man," Molly looked at him, horrified. "I can only imagine what they'd end up with, but I'm sure it would have beef jerky in it."

Greg laughed. She was probably right. Greg wasn't the best at organizing gifts or gift baskets.

"I'll gladly leave that up to you," Greg bowed.

"That's settled then," Molly said. "Now, I need to get changed so I can go see what we're going to have for dinner."

"I'm sure myself and Tammy can sort that out!" Greg's eyebrows shot up at the look of horror that filled Molly's eyes when he said that.

"My dear boy, I have never tasted your cooking, but believe me, I've tasted Tammy's," Molly explained. "While my niece is a star at many things, cooking is not one of those things."

"Oh!" Greg nodded in understanding. "Well, then she and I have that in common."

"Then it's agreed that I do the cooking while I'm here, and I'll hear none of this nonsense about take-out," Molly told him.

"Sorry to interrupt," Jude butted in. "But can we chat in about half an hour? I have to go and look at my apartment now."

"Yes, we're taking Jude to go see where he's living," Brynn told them.

"Sure," Greg nodded. "Go ahead. We'll catch up later."

Greg watched as Maggie, Brynn, and Jude left the room.

"They do love him, don't they?" Molly watched them disappear, followed by three basset hounds. "It looks as if you've lost your fur babies, my dear." She turned to Tammy.

"They love being around the kids," Tammy agreed. "I can't say I blame them. I think I'm totally boring compared to the excitement they have with the girls."

"I, for one, am glad the kids have the bassets." Greg looked at her. Their eyes met and held for a brief second. His heart jolted when he saw a glimpse of the Tammy he used to know shining in their depths.

Chapter Twelve

IT'S NOT THAT EASY TO PUT THE PAST BEHIND YOU

It had been five days since Brett Parker had been shot. It had also been five days since Constance had admitted to playing a part in what had happened on Double A the day Tammy arrived. Another five-day milestone was her and Greg being able to get along having teamed up to look into Brian's death and the incidents on the ranches. To avoid raising suspicions, Tammy and Greg were careful to keep up the appearance of disliking each other. That wasn't the hard part because Tammy still harbored ill feelings towards the man. While she trusted him in their joined task force they'd formed, Tammy would never trust him with her heart ever again.

In the last five days of putting their heads together, they'd been able to find out that there was someone who could help them find out about the avalanche. She was a visitor at Cupids Bow Ranch and had worked with a team of experts studying avalanches. Greg had asked Jane to come and meet them later that afternoon. Tammy had spoken with the young woman on the phone. She seemed rather excited to go on a trip to the exclusive resort and was more than confident that she'd be able to get in. It had been shut since the accident six months ago. Tammy was waiting for the resort owner to get back to her so they could make the arrangements.

Tammy was more than sure the resort owners would also like to get to the bottom of what happened. When she'd first spoken to them a few days after the avalanche, they'd seemed as shocked by what had happened as everyone else. The resort had an impeccable safety record and did constant checks before opening the ski runs each day. As far as the owners were concerned, there were no indications that it would happen. There were constant checks of the runs throughout the day as well. The resort catered to high-profile clientele and couldn't take any chances with risk factors such as those. Tammy had been surprised that both she and Greg had the same thought about Brian's accidents at the resort. It didn't make any sense, and the resort was now under scrutiny with court cases for negligence, failing compliance, and a whole lot of other trouble.

Tammy had made it clear to the resort that she wasn't looking to sue them; she was looking to find out what had happened and thought that maybe their findings would end up helping the resort, especially if the avalanche had been intentionally caused. The expert Tammy was sending would also be at Tammy's expense, and not the resort's. Tammy was sure by now the ski resort was starting to feel the pressure of having been shut down. They didn't know for sure yet whether they'd be able to open for the season this year or not, even though the town had a constant stream of tourists because, even in summer, the resort's nature trails were something to behold. The small town that serviced the resort also benefitted from them. So, Tammy's investigation could potentially save an entire town from dying out. At least that's the pitch Tammy had used when she'd left a message for the resort owner earlier.

In the meantime, while they were waiting to get that part of their investigation going, Tammy and Greg had to attend a ranch meeting at Double A ranch. Brett Anderson was getting out of the hospital today and had called a meeting for some reason. Greg said he thought he knew what it was about but would rather Tammy found out at the meeting. Tammy's Uncle Robert and Aunt Molly were still at Double A, but Robert spent most of his days at the sheriff's office, where Constance was still being held.

Tammy knew that, between the sheriff and Robert, Constance was in a cell on her own. They'd put up curtains to make her more comfortable and afford her some privacy. They had also given Constance a lot of other comforts like a decent mattress, pillows, and so on. Tammy was still furious with Constance, and her head reeled with disbelief that she could've betrayed them as she had. But that didn't mean she wanted Constance locked in a cell with hardened criminals. Tammy was glad they were in a small town and the Sheriff could do what he'd done for her while she was being detained. From what Aunt Molly had told Tammy, Constance didn't know that Pete and his gang were going to steal the animals. Constance certainly did not know about the kidnapping plan; she would have never condoned them taking Maggie.

Pete had told Constance that they only wanted to scare the ranches and let them feel what losing their jobs would feel like to them. Most of them had worked this land straight out of school. There were rumors that the ranches were going bankrupt, and soon there would be heavy layoffs. The ranch hands and other staff on the ranches were told that all five ranches were in the process of being sold to a land development company – because some of the other ranches that bordered them were also selling out. The land developers buying up the land were no longer using it as ranch land but were turning it into housing complexes and shopping malls. None of that was true, and from what Tammy knew, all the ranch owners had assured their staff those were just rumors.

Robert and the Sheriff had learned that there were some fraudulent land deeds in circulation, showing that Brian and Chelsea had already signed the deals. That is why their lands had been hit the hardest. But Tammy knew that Brian hadn't signed or sold their farm. He couldn't do that without Tammy's knowledge or signature. Robert had spoken to Chelsea and she had no such knowledge either, but it was worrying that those papers were in circulation. According to Pete, his brother told him that it was only a matter of time before Zac Sparrow signed his deal. Which was ludicrous because Zac had big plans for Cupids Bow and was trying to get the other four ranches to move in the same direction. At first, Tammy wasn't sure she'd want to turn the ranch into a country inn. But after mentioning it to Brynn and Maggie, and, she couldn't believe she'd done it, Greg too, they'd all seem keen on the idea.

Tammy looked at her wristwatch. She had to get to that meeting at Big Valley. Tammy's day was rather full as after that, she had to meet with Jane, the new housekeeper she and Greg were interviewing. That silly knot tightened in her stomach at the thought of Greg, and her heart did a little skip. Tammy chose to ignore it but soon found the knot turning into a flutter and her heart picked up speed when he appeared at the study door.

"You ready to go?" Greg asked her, looming in the doorway. His six-foot-three frame made the entry seem small. His broad shoulders were outlined by his dark blue western shirt rolled up to the elbows. The shirt was tucked into his faded, retrofit, boot-cut jeans hanging over his dark boots. The waistband of his jeans rode his hips and was held up by a leather belt with a silver buckle. His long, lean masculine fingers played with his well-worn black Stetson he held between them. Tammy swallowed as her throat went dry and her pulse picked up speed.

This is going to be a long afternoon! Tammy sighed to herself, fighting to get her rebellious heart under control. She and Greg Watson were not happening; not in this lifetime or any other, as far as Tammy was concerned. Admittedly, she'd enjoyed working with him over these past few days. They'd even worked out a silent truce over Greg now being a one-quarter owner of Double A Ranch. But that is as far as it was ever going to go between the two of them. They'd tried the relationship route once before, and things went south before they'd even had a chance to get off the starting line. Greg had been her first love, and he had shattered her young heart into tiny shards.

Tammy was no longer a lovesick teenager, and she really didn't want to have to pick up any more pieces at this stage of her life. She'd already lost too much, been lied to enough, and walked over far too many times by the men she'd been foolish enough to give her heart to. Once all the trouble with the land and getting to the bottom of Brian's death was over, Tammy was going to kick back and enjoy her retirement while working the ranch. She was also planning on being the best parent to Brynn that she could be. Tammy now had to be both mother and father to her niece, so there was no place in her life for anyone else. Brynn needed Tammy to be all in for her, and that is what Tammy was going to be.

"Tammy?" Greg's deep voice pulled Tammy from her musings, making her cheeks heat up when she realized she'd been staring at him.

"Sorry, I was thinking about Brynn," Tammy said. "Are you sure it's okay to leave her and Maggie here with just Amy?"

"Jude will be back in twenty minutes with Molly, and he has the two new men Wallace sent keeping an eye out for the three of them," Greg assured her, "I vetted those other men from the security agency myself, and they are good men."

"I know," Tammy sighed. "I just worry about them. Especially Maggie, after what she went through."

"I do, too," Greg told her. "But she's in good hands this time, and Brett insisted there be no younger generation at the meeting."

Tammy and Greg left Double A in two separate vehicles. When they arrived at Big Valley, they kept their distance, even though Tammy found herself seeking him out the entire time. She had to force herself to concentrate on the room full of people. As far as Tammy and Greg knew, no one outside of Double A and the Sheriff knew about Constance yet. Greg and Tammy had agreed to keep it that way until Robert had sorted a few things out and the police had finished interrogating Pete's gang.

When Tammy walked into the living room where the

meeting was being held, she noted that Maria, Cat, Chelsea, and Ashley were all seated on a large sofa. Greg had gone to sit in front of the large fireplace with Zac, West, and Brett. Their seats had been arranged to face the rest of the people in the room. Tammy took a seat in one of the plush chairs next to Chelsea, who smiled in greeting at her when she sat down. Tammy noted that Ryan Beckett had taken a seat on the opposite side of the sofa next to Maria. He was fidgeting with a laptop. A few minutes after they were all seated, the front door opened. Wallace Black, Cat's bodyguard, and Janine Tanner, the Cupids Bow Inn manager, slipped into the room.

The coffee table was ladened with snacks, and the side table at the back of the room had urns of hot water, tea, coffee, milk, cream, sugar, water, and soft drinks on it. Sylvie, the Parkers' housekeeper, had laid out quite the spread for the meeting. She was also one of the best cooks in the entire valley, and Tammy wished she could get a housekeeper as good as her. Or as good as... Tammy swallowed and took a silent breath to stamp away from the hurt and sorrow she felt every time she thought of Constance. She was even battling with interviewing to fill Constance's position. Tammy felt like she was betraying her somehow, which was nonsense because Constance had betrayed her. The anger quickly sprung up, washing away the feelings of guilt, hurt, and sorrow.

Before Tammy could think about Constance again, Brett started to speak.

"We're just waiting for David and Gwen," Brett told them and looked at Ryan. "Have you managed to get your sister on Zoom or Skype?"

"Yes, she's just turning off her phone." Ryan turned the laptop towards where Brett and the other three men were sitting.

"Hi," Gwen's voice echoed from the computer.

Everyone greeted her back. Ryan held the laptop up so everyone could see Gwen.

No sooner had Ryan put the laptop onto his lap facing Brett,

Zac, West, and Greg than the front door once again opened, and boots were heard walking into the room. Tammy turned around to see David Miller walk in. She noted his eyes go immediately to Cat's and a slight pink stain on Cat's cheek as she smiled up at him. It was good to see Cat happy again. Heavens knew she deserved it after everything she'd been through with both of her ex-husbands. Tammy's heart went out to her. She also hoped that David Miller would realize what a treasure he had in Cat and treat her right. Tammy made a mental note to have a word with the mysterious David Miller as soon as the opportunity arose.

They may not have been that close, as Tammy was three years older than them, but they were like family. Even if there'd been some weird family feud between the five families, they all still looked out for each other. Callum Sparrow was a firm believer in helping your friends, neighbors, and kin no matter how mad you were at them. He seemed to have instilled that in all five families because no matter what when someone needed a hand, everyone in the valley pitched in. Tammy glanced around the room and realized she wasn't the only one that had noticed the exchange between them. Zac and West seemed to be the most concerned by the way their eyes had narrowed warningly at David.

"Sorry, I'm late," David said, ignoring the steely stares. "I was delivering the last of your new horses." His eyes slid towards Chelsea.

"Thank you, David," Chelsea's voice filled with emotion, and her eyes misted over.

Tammy felt that silly lump in her throat rise once again. She'd forgotten that feeling. The one that said you were never really alone; there was always someone to reach out to, no matter what. Right now, all the ranches were chipping in to help Chelsea get back on her feet. After David nodded and tipped his hat a Chelsea, he took the only available seat next to Tammy.

"Are they all secure?" Zac asked David, who nodded. "You've allocated the men to guard the ranch?"

"Yes, it is all taken care of," David assured him and looked at

Wallace. "Wallace has brought in more security from his firm to help out, and they all arrived with the horses."

"Good!" Zac nodded and gave Chelsea a warm smile. "We need to make sure this doesn't happen again."

Tammy was starting to feel a little bit uncomfortable with all the love that seemed to be in the air. Zac and Chelsea could hardly take their eyes off each other as well. Wallace and Janine didn't think anyone noticed their legs touching at the knees. Then, there were the coveted glances between West and Maria.

Oh, for goodness' sake! Tammy thought. It was like being in some teen movie where all the love-struck teens were making googly eyes at each other. Without thinking, her eyes automatically swung to Greg's, and she caught him quickly averting his gaze. *Was he staring at me?*

Tammy breathed a sigh of relief when Janine started to talk.

"Yes, but I still say you should've waited until after all this was cleared up before getting more animals," Janine pointed out. "Aren't they just new targets for the thugs to steal?"

"We're counting on it!" Wallace smiled at Janine.

Oh no! That doesn't sound good! Tammy's eyes slid to Wallace. There was something in the smile, raised eyebrow, and the glint in his eyes that told her more trouble was fast approaching. This time, though, they were luring the trouble to them like a fisherman chumming the waters to catch a shark. Tammy wasn't too sure how she felt about baiting their invisible foes, especially knowing what they were capable of and not knowing how far they would go.

Tammy's mind was taken away from Wallace when Brett started the meeting.

"I know you're all wondering why I've called this meeting," Brett began and looked at Ashley. "I'm sorry Billy couldn't make it, but he said you had complete control over plans for the ranch, is that correct?"

"Yes," Ashley said.

Something in her voice caught Tammy's attention, and she turned to see Ashley's eyes narrow. She was clearly not happy with the way Brett had worded his question. Tammy couldn't blame her, really. Brett had sounded quite condescending as if Ashley was just a wife who'd been given temporary permission to speak on behalf of her master.

Tammy knew that Brett had probably not meant it to sound the way it had come out, but he'd got Ashley's back up. She remembered Ashley telling her how hard it had been for her to gain control of her father's law firm. His staff had tried to walk all over her, making her feel as if she hadn't earned the position handed to her. But she'd worked for it all right and paid her dues to sit in her father's chair. Rupert Cuthbert would never have handed over the reins if he'd felt his daughter hadn't earned her seat or was ready. Ashley still got a lot of flak from some of the lawyers who worked at the firm, but she'd learned fast how to deal with them. Still, sometimes it got to Ashley, and she didn't need it from her friends or their brothers as well.

"Great," Brett said, totally oblivious to the look Ashley shot at him as he looked at Zac.

"A couple of weeks ago, Janine was told and not asked that an event was to be held at Cupids Bow Ranch," Zac took over the meeting. "As you all know, I've been asking about your ranches, helping out with accommodation. We've now all talked about restructuring your homesteads into country inns to boost your revenue and help us all keep our lands."

"Thank you for responding so positively to the request for helping out with accommodations," Janine told them before leaning forward to look pointedly at Tammy and then Ryan. "Please don't forget to submit the quotes for any renovations or items you're going to need to accommodate these picky guests to me before the end of today."

"Sure," Tammy said at the same time as Greg.

Her head shot around to look at him, and their eye collided. Tammy's heart leaped into her throat as the gold in his eyes seemed to sparkle at her. She quickly looked away, jumping with fright when Brett's voice seemed to boom and echo through the room.

"Maria!" Brett's eyes narrowed in on Chelsea angrily grabbing the four woman's attention. "What are you four discussing that's so important?"

"She doesn't have to answer that," Ashley told him, holding his stare without flinching. "She's not a teenager."

"Brett," West said to him before he leaned over and whispered something to Brett, who nodded.

"I know we told you that you'll be hosting celebrity guests, but we haven't told you much more about the event," Brett continued, his eyes slowly touching everyone in the room as he spoke. "There was a reason for that."

"As you know, all the guests will be some sort of celebrity guest," Zac picked up where Brett left off. "We needed to keep their names on the quiet right until they are about to arrive to avoid any leaks to the press."

"If we are all going to become country inns and want to attract this level of clientele, we have to learn to do things this way." West stepped in and looked over to Wallace. "Wallace will be heading up security for the entire event."

"Ryan, I know you're one of the owners," Wallace leaned forward and looked at Ryan. "But with your background, I'd appreciate it if you could lend me a hand. You know this land better than I do or anyone else, I believe."

"Sure." Ryan nodded.

"I'll be back tomorrow," Gwen's voice came from the computer, "so Ryan will have time to help you, Wallace."

"Thank you, mam," Wallace said, lifting his hat politely at the screen Ryan held towards Wallace.

"What is the event for, Zac?" Gwen asked Zac and Ryan pointed the computer housing Gwen's face at him.

"It's for a celebrity engagement party," Zac told Gwen.

Oh, no! Tammy thought, knowing fully well how many of those big events went down. Not to mention that no matter how much one tried, the press would always get wind of it. The last thing any of the ranches needed right now was a swarm of paparazzi buzzing around.

"Do we know this celebrity?" Gwen asked him.

Tammy turned and looked at Zac. She was about to ask that same question.

"I think you were at his first marriage?" Zac said, and his eyes darted to Cat.

Cold crept up Tammy's spine as she looked around at Cat before sliding back to Zac while it dawned on her who Zac was talking about.

"Are you talking about who I think you are?" Tammy asked, jumping in before Cat could ask. "Because if you are, I think that is completely out of order, and I'm rethinking offering my home to their guests."

Tammy looked around at Cat, giving her a warm, supportive smile.

"What's going on, Zac?" Cat's eyes narrowed as she looked at her older brother. "Who are you all referring to?"

"I'm sorry, Kitty Cat," Zac's voice dropped. "It's Paul's."

"My ex-husband, Paul?" Cat's face resonated with shock, and Tammy's heart went out to her.

Chapter Thirteen
FROM VICTIM TO SUSPECT

Tammy couldn't believe her ears. Her first thought was how the heck Zac could agree to let Cat's ex-husband have his engagement at Cupids Bow? The man was rubbing salt in Cat's wounds and disturbing the sacred space that was her home. Tammy would freak out if that had been Martin. It was one thing catching him cheating on her in their home in LA, but if it had been at Double A, that would've shattered the last bit of peace Tammy had in her heart: her sacred part of this world, her home.

"Yes," David said, leaning forward to look at Cat, "Zac told me this morning. I'm so sorry I didn't come and tell you right away to prepare you." Tammy knew she saw the look of genuine concern in his eyes that David cared deeply for Cat. "But Zac made me promise not to because he wanted to tell you himself."

Tammy also knew that it had hurt David not to have ridden straight out to tell Cat as soon as he found out. While she felt awful for Cat about what her ex-husband was doing to her, Tammy's heart filled with joy for Cat to have found David.

"It's okay, David." Cat gave him a warm smile. "I'm not mad at you. I know Zac would've kept this from you because we've been working so closely together these past weeks." She turned her head to look at her brother. Her eyes were icy. "How long have you known about this?"

Tammy knew that's what they all wanted to know.

"Since the day after Paul faxed the guest list and then the order for the event," Zac hedged.

"How long, Zac?" Cat's tone of voice spoke volumes, resonating with hurt and anger at her brother.

"Almost four weeks," Janine was the one to answer the question and not Zac.

"Four weeks?" Maria, Cat, Chelsea, and Ashley said altogether, all four heads turning to Janine before swiveling back to Zac for confirmation.

"So, you've all known since before Paul left the ranch to go for his audition?" Ashley's narrowed eyes scanned across Zac, Brett, Greg, and then West before leaning forward to look towards Janine.

"I knew," Janine said, correcting Ashley. "Zac didn't know until after Paul was gone."

"And you, Wallace?" Ashley looked at him

"I didn't know until a couple of weeks ago," Wallace answered her without hesitation, but Tammy picked up a trace of guilt in his voice.

"Wallace really didn't know," Janine defended him diligently. "Only I did until a few weeks ago when the money for the entire event was cleared in the Cupids Bow Inn bank account."

Wow, Janine was really throwing herself under the bus for these men! Tammy gave a soft sigh and shook her head, glancing over at the four men in front of her. None of them were doing anything to help her out either.

"Really?" Ashley's tone stated her disbelief in what Janine had just said.

"Yes," Janine stubbornly stuck to her story. "I knew Zac did daily bank checks, and he'd spot that amount of money in the account and question it."

"Uh-huh," was all Ashley said to that while she nodded. Her

expression was blank, and Tammy knew that Ashley was not someone you wanted to play poker with.

"Chelsea," Ashley turned her attention to the woman sitting on her left. "Who do all the venue bookings have to go through at Cupids Bow Inn before the..." She paused and looked at Janine, "Inn's manager can approve them and give the party wanting to book the venue a definite answer?"

"It used to be me when I was still living at Cupids Bow," Chelsea told Ashley, and Tammy could see how nervous Chelsea looked under Ashley's watchful eyes.

"I'm asking about now," Ashley pointed out. "Who passes them now that you no longer do?"

"Only Zac can do that," Chelsea's voice dropped, and her eyes darted to Zac.

"So, Janine, that tells me you're lying to us." Ashley looked directly at Janine. "Not only you are not very good at lying, but you also have a terrible tell. Do you know that your hands started to shake the moment you threw yourself under the bus for Zac?"

"This is not a courtroom interrogation, Ashley," Brett stepped in, rushing to Zac and Janine's rescue. "We've brought you all here to tell you about the event, not point fingers of blame for keeping secrets."

"If you're keeping this from us, Brett, it makes us all wonder what else the four of you are hiding." Ashley's narrowed eyes and smug smile were directed at the four men sitting in front of them.

All the heads on Tammy's side of the room turned towards the four men on the other side of the room. Tammy could've sworn she'd seen a moment's panic flash in all four of their eyes, which made her wonder the same thing. What else were those four keeping from them? More importantly, did it have something to do with what was going on at the ranches or even her brother's death?

"What is your interrogation really about, Ashley?" Greg, who up until now had said nothing, looked at Ashley with narrowed suspicious eyes and asked.

"You tell me." Ashley returned the narrow steely look.

For someone so tiny, she was pretty mighty, and Tammy was glad that Ashley was now her lawyer. She reminded Tammy of what Uncle Robert used to be like in his day, and, at that moment, Tammy knew all her affairs were in good hands with Ashley. Nothing escaped those shrewd, seeking eyes of her.

"Because the four of you..." Ashley continued after a brief pause of staring down at Greg. She used her index finger to point at the four men facing them, "Look really guilty right now."

"Guilty for what?" Greg challenged her. "Keeping an engagement event of Cat's ex-husband to West's ex-wife a secret?"

"Excuse me?" Cat, Tammy, and Gwen all hissed at the same time.

"I'm sorry, Cat." Wests looked directly at Cat, and Tammy could see the conflict in his eyes. "It seems that Astrid and Paul have deliberately picked Cupids Bow to have their engagement party at to torment us both."

"It's not just to torment you," Zac said, looking at his sister, Cat before his eyes slid to Janine. He nodded. "We think it's to publicly humiliate you, West, and Maria."

"Me?" Maria looked up. Her eyes held surprise. "She's already done that to me. Well, she didn't humiliate me, but she turned me into some black widow husband murderer."

"She's also divulged yours, Cat's, West's, and..." Zac looked at Tammy. "Tammy's whereabouts."

It was Tammy's turn to look shocked as she gaped at Zac in confusion. She hardly knew Paul or Astrid. Tammy had refused to let her firm take their cases to sort out their images after what they had done to Cat and West. So, Tammy wasn't sure what grudge they'd have against her.

"Why would Astrid or Paul care about my whereabouts?" Tammy asked, a little confused.

"Because there are questions over your late husband's death," West told Tammy. "I'm so sorry, Tam."

Tammy heard Maria's quick intake of breath, and she barely glanced around at her as she looked back at West. She barely heard Maria stand up and excuse herself from the room. Her mind was spinning around what West had just said.

"I'm not sure I understand," Tammy told West. "I don't know much about Martin's death, and all I was told is that he broke his neck when he tumbled as the snow hit him."

She knew that was a rather gruesome thing to blurt out casually, but Tammy's mind was reeling right now. Not over the questions about the circumstances that led to Martin's death – because Tammy and Greg also thought those were strange. But the accusation in West's voice meant that people thought she had something to do with it.

"I found out today, Tammy, that the FBI is looking for you to question you and your uncle Robert," Greg's voice caused Tammy's head to snap around to look at him.

"When did you learn about this?" Tammy's voice had dropped to a whisper as she looked at Greg.

"I told him when he got here," West told her.

Tammy nodded as a strange, surreal feeling washed over her. A warm hand touched her arm, and she turned towards it. Ashley had swapped places with Chelsea on the sofa, and she was leaning towards her.

"Tammy, you don't say a word to anyone who asks you questions until I'm by your side," Ashley told her and looked over towards the four men. "You don't even speak to anyone outside this room, okay?"

Tammy couldn't believe what was happening. How did she suddenly go from being a victim of Martin's crimes to basically being accused of murdering him? Tammy's eyes held Ashley's, but, at the moment, she couldn't find her voice, so she nodded.

"Good," Ashley smiled encouragingly at her. "I'll make some calls and find out what is going on. I know someone who can help us with that."

Once again, all Tammy could do was nod.

"Now, are we finished with this meeting?" Ashley gave

Tammy's arm a comforting squeeze before letting it go to address the room.

"Well, we did want to discuss the way forward with the event," Zac told her.

"The event is canceled," Ashley told them in no uncertain terms before turning to Janine. "You will make the call this afternoon and tell Paul that, due to unforeseen circumstances, all events are canceled until further notice."

"But we've already spent almost half of the deposit getting things ready–" before Janine could finish, Ashley cut her off.

"Deposits are usually non-refundable. If they have an issue with that, send them to me," Ashley told her. "Pay back the half you still have, pack up the rest of Paul's things he left at the ranch, and have them sent back to him."

"Wait a minute!" Zac's voice was laced with anger. "You can't just go doing that!"

"I can, and I just have," Ashley told him. "I can also get law enforcement in here within a few minutes to declare all our ranches unfit for visitors until the trouble has been cleared up. You see, right now, Zac, you are knowingly putting your guests in danger."

"I am not!" Zac hissed.

"Are you aware of all the trouble that's been happening on the ranches?" Ashley asked him.

"Of course, we all are!" Zac suddenly realized what he'd said, and his jaw clenched. "There's not been any trouble at Cupids Bow."

"No?" Ashley looked at him with raised eyebrows. "So, Cat wasn't shot at? David wasn't actually shot either, and you were not beaten up on Cupids Bow not too long ago while you had guests?"

"I..." Zac's eyes narrowed, and he glared at Ashley.

"There you go," Ashley pointed out. "Cancel the event!" She said in no uncertain terms, "Or you will leave me with no other choice but to call in the authorities. Then I will speak to each of your current guests and represent them too."

"What has gotten into you, Ashley?" Brett's eyes mirrored Zac's anger. "Why would you do this to us?"

"Why would any of you even entertain the idea of holding an event that would clearly be a witch hunt on any of our properties?" Ashley hit the question back. "I find that so insensitive. Both of your sisters are here trying to get over what happened to them." She turned to Tammy. "Tammy has had the most recent loss and has had to deal with one shock after the other since getting back here."

"I have to agree with Ashley," Chelsea said. "I'm sorry, I want to run a country inn too, but right now is not the best time." She looked at Janine. "Janine is right. Everything we try to build, rebuild, or replace right now is just extra costs for whoever our enemy is to tear down once again."

"I'll cancel the event and gets Paul's belongings back to him as soon as I get back to the ranch," Janine promised Ashley.

"Janine, I did not authorize that!" Zac hissed.

"No, but I am," Cat spoke up. "You may as well all know that I'm the full owner of Cupids Bow. It's a long story, one I don't have time to get into right now as my friend, Maria, needs me." She looked at Zac. "I say no event!"

"I second that," Ryan spoke up.

"I say no event as well," Gwen's voice echoed through the laptop.

"I agree with them," Tammy finally found her voice, even though it was a bit croaky.

"You all realize that all our ranches need the cash flow this event could bring us?" Brett said in exasperation.

"We'll find it another way," Gwen told him.

"I don't have a lot left after what Martin did to me," Tammy said softly. "But whatever capital I have, I will put into helping all of us."

"I will do the same," Cat said.

"I can pad that with proceeds from my cosmetic company sale," Gwen said.

"I have some savings," Ryan said.

"I can help out as well," David put up his hand.

Tammy felt a lump growing in her throat once again as she watched the neighbors all coming together to join forces and pitch in.

"I guess that's settled then," Ashley turned to Zac and Brett. "If Paul or Astrid try and give you problems, let me know. I'll waiver all fees to represent all the ranches for any repercussions over the canceled event or fall out over the problems we're having right now."

"Thank you, Ashley," Brett said, looking relieved. "We may need you for something much more serious than that."

All eyes shot to Brett, but he didn't elaborate on what he meant. He just sat back and rubbed a hand over his face as if he'd just been defeated.

"Can we have a word with you in private, please, Tammy?" Cat leaned forward to look at her.

"Sure," Tammy nodded and stood up.

Cat, Chelsea, Ashley, and Tammy didn't bother to excuse themselves as they left the room. The meeting was over as far as they were concerned. Tammy followed the three women into the study.

"What is going on with you and West?" Cat blurted out before Ashley had fully closed the door.

Tammy stood staring at Cat in shock. Was she being accused of something else here?

"You think West and I..." Tammy looked at them as it dawned on her that they thought she had a romantic relationship with West.

She stared wide-eyed at the three women staring back at her, and suddenly it seemed rather funny to her. Today Tammy had been accused of having something to do with Martin's death and now of being romantically involved with a very good friend of hers. She couldn't stop the grin that spread across her lips or the laughter that bubbled up, escaping before she could stop it.

"I'm sorry," Tammy said, raising her hand as she swallowed

down her laughter. "It's just been such a surreal past few days since I arrived back in Montana."

"Tell us about it!" Cat sighed, her lips starting to twitch as well.

"Cat!" both Ashley and Chelsea warned her.

"I'm sorry, but you know how catchy laughter is to me," Cat pursed her lips as her belly started to jiggle with suppressed laughter.

"So, you and West were never romantically involved?" Ashley's eyes shone with mirth, but she was much better at controlling it than Tammy, Cat, and even Chelsea, who was biting her lips and trying not to laugh.

All Tammy could do was shake her head in denial.

"I don't mean to sound like we're in high school here." Ashley swallowed and cleared her throat. "But do you think you could pretend you noticed how upset Maria was and then come up to explain this to her?" She cleared her throat again. "West is the first man in a long, long time that Maria has started to let in."

That last sentence of Ashley worked in clearing away the funny as everyone knew in some form or other about the tragedy of Maria's husband's death.

"Of course," Tammy agreed right away, clearing her throat and gathering herself.

"Thank you," Cat said as she, Ashley, and Chelsea left the study.

Tammy stood watching the empty doorway for a few minutes before looking at her watch. She didn't have a lot of time left before she had to be back at Double A, but this was important to Maria, so Tammy's appointment would have to wait a bit.

Tammy gave it ten minutes before making her way up the stairs, hoping that Maria was still in the same room she'd been in when they were younger. As she topped the stairs, she frowned, seeing a figure in a dark hoodie rush down the back stairs that led to the kitchen. A shudder ran down Tammy's spine, but she was probably being paranoid, and it was one of the Big Valley's staff.

Tammy heard voices coming from the room that she'd known as Maria's when they were younger and was glad to find it was still Maria's room. The door was slightly open, so Tammy stood listening while waiting for an appropriate time to enter and make her presence known. She found the right moment and stepped into Maria's room. Once in there, Tammy assured Maria that nothing was going on between herself and West. She also told her that they'd been friends since they were young, and he used to come to visit Cupids bow with Cat's aunt Simone.

Tammy was surprised to find out that they didn't seem to know West, nor did they know about the fatal accident that nearly ended his life. It wasn't the night of Tammy, Zac, and Brett's prom when the three men were involved in a car accident with a few others. Once again, Tammy had been surprised that none of the four women had known about that either, especially when both Cat and Maria's brothers were also nearly fatally injured. It was not the best night for Tammy either and was one she'd spent years trying to forget.

Before she could tell them about the accident West had interrupted them with an alarming message that Tammy and Greg were needed back at Double A. There was someone there to see Tammy. She was now thinking it was not the new housekeeper or Jane. Tammy had handled many police and FBI agents in her time, dealing with the high-profile celebrities that she dealt with on a daily basis back in LA. But an investigation had never involved her personally. Tammy did feel a bit better after watching Ashley in action in a friendly meeting. She could only imagine what the little spitfire would be like in a real case scenario. It was also a little strange to Tammy that the minute she and Greg had started looking into the avalanche, an investigation had opened.

Tammy shook her head and sighed as she drove back to Double A. So much for a nice peaceful retirement! As she pulled into the ranch, her heart lurched. Two black SUVs were parked in front of her house. They looked like standard-issue government vehicles to her. She drove around to the garages and noted that all the cars, including her Uncle Robert's hire, were parked there. Everyone was home except Greg. Tammy felt a little better that Robert was there, even though she was still furious with him.

Tammy parked and climbed out of the car. She noticed Jude, Amy, and the kids were saddling up some of the horses. They waved to her when they saw her. Tammy waved back and turned as Greg's car pulled up next to hers. She stood and waited for Greg to catch up to her.

"I think the FBI is here," Tammy told him. "Not sure why there are two FBI cars though."

"One of them belongs to Wallace," Greg said. "He got wind of who was on the way to the ranch, and that is why he left Big Valley ranch in such a hurry. Wallace wanted to be here when the agents arrived."

"Why?" Tammy asked, her brows creasing into a frown. "What has this got to do with Wallace?"

"He said he'd explain everything to us later and that I should be here with you," Greg told her.

"Thank you," Tammy said and gave Greg a grateful smile. "I feel better with all of you here, even Uncle Robert."

"Of course," Greg smiled back. "I would never let you face whatever this witch hunt is on your own." His eyes sought hers. "We're partners remember?" His voice dropped.

Tammy stood staring into Greg's unusual green-gold eyes and felt herself being drawn in. Someone cleared their throat from behind her, making them break eye contact and Tammy spin around. Wallace was standing behind her.

"Are the two of you investigating the avalanche at that exclusive ski resort?" Wallace asked them.

"Yes, why?" Greg looked at Wallace questioningly.

"You seemed to have ruffled feathers and sparked some interest in why you are doing that," Wallace told them. "Before we go in there, care to give me a brief overview?" He looked from Tammy to Greg. "I'm only asking so I can help you both out here and actually help you with your investigation as well."

Before Greg could answer him, Tammy did and gave Wallace a quick rundown as to hers and Greg's suspicions.

"You should've come to me right away," Wallace told them. "I can help with that. You know Indy's friend Jane? Her father is here."

"Why would he be here?" Greg asked, his brow furrowing into a confused frown.

"He's the lead agent on the case," Wallace explained. "Apparently, Jane contacted him to ask if he knew of any suspected foul play that could've caused the avalanche."

"Jane's father is FBI?" Tammy asked, surprised. "Well, this just gets better and better."

"Robert told me about your husband and gave me an overview of your situation," Wallace admitted to Tammy. "I'm sorry to have to pry, but I'm on your side, and I needed to know a few things before those agents arrived."

"Okay!" Tammy gave Wallace a sideways look.

"Let's go." Wallace turned to start walking inside.

"Greg is going to stay with me, though, right?" Tammy suddenly didn't want to face the FBI on her own.

"Let them try and stop me," Greg said, stepping closer to Tammy and taking her hand. "Partners, remember?" he said into her ear before gently pulling her inside.

EPILOGUE

Tammy had just hung her hat and coat on the rack when her uncle popped out of the living room.

"Hello, Tammy. Please, come in here," Robert said. His stiff posture alerted her that he was in his lawyer mode. "There are some FBI agents that would like to ask you a few questions about the avalanche."

"Sure," Tammy said, turning to look at Wallace and Greg. "But they are coming with me."

Robert looked at the two men, and she saw the smile he exchanged with them before nodding, "Of course."

Robert stepped aside and let Tammy walk into the room ahead of him.

"Mrs. Guest?" the man that was her height stood up and walked over to her. "I'm Agent Jess Yates, and this is my partner, Agent Sarah Dodd."

"It's actually Ms. Anderson. I never took my husband's surname," Tammy told them. "But please, call me Tammy."

"Right," Agent Yates said. "Thank you for coming back to the ranch so soon, and we're sorry to drop in unannounced like this."

"No, you're not," Wallace said, stepping up next to Tammy. "Shall we take a seat and get this over with?"

"Agent Black," Agent Yates looked at Wallace. "As we've already explained, we are simply trying to find out what Ms. Anderson knows about the avalanche."

"No, you're on a fishing expedition to try and pin the avalanche on someone because someone got wind of Ms. Anderson and Mr. Watson's investigation into it." Wallace guided Tammy to a sofa. When Tammy sat down, Wallace sat on one side of her and Greg on the other. "Now you have some very high-profile people wanting to know what the heck is going on."

"Is this true?" Robert took a seat next to the sofa facing the two agents who sat together on the second sofa in the room.

"No, we simply wanted to know why Ms. Anderson and Mr. Watson are digging into the avalanche incident," Agent Dodds insisted. "It is quite alarming if there is any truth at all that the avalanche had been deliberate, and that would be a case for the FBI."

"Are you warning us off?" Tammy suddenly realized why the agents were at her door. They weren't here to interrogate her or point fingers at her as a suspect in the death of Martin. They were here to warn Tammy and Greg away from digging further into the matter. "What is really going on here?"

"It would be in your own best interests to leave the investigating to the experts, Ms. Anderson," Agent Yates said. "I also do not want my daughter getting involved in this. If someone did, and I'm neither denying nor verifying this, deliberately start an avalanche, they are not the type of people you want to be messing around with."

"So, you do suspect foul play?" Tammy's eyes narrowed.

"We did not say that Ms. Anderson," Agent Dodds said. "What we can tell you is that we have an ongoing investigation into the matter."

Tammy was about to say more when the doorbell rang.

"I'll get it," Molly's voice rang out down the hallway.

"So, then, you came all this way to warn us to stop looking into the avalanche?" Tammy's brows shot up in surprise.

"Excuse me," Molly walked into the room. "Tammy, may I have a word, please?"

Tammy nodded and stood up, "Excuse me." She walked to the door and followed Molly down the hall to the study.

"Who was at the door?" Tammy said softly.

"Your visitor," Molly told her, stopping at the door to the study.

"Who..." Tammy stepped around Molly and stopped at the doorway. "Jane?"

Molly stepped back into the hallway and pulled the study door closed behind her.

"I'm so sorry that I alerted my father," Jane told her. Tammy noticed she was clutching a file she had stuffed under her arm.

"I know you didn't do it deliberately and were only trying to help us," Tammy told her.

"I did some digging into that day of the avalanche," Jane told her. "I've sent a whole lot of messages and videos to your phone. I found them on various social media accounts of some of the survivors at the resort on that day."

"I don't have my phone," Tammy told her.

"That's okay." Jane pulled her bag off her shoulder, plopped the file from under her arm on the desk, and took her laptop out of the bag. "Here, I'll show you."

Tammy leaned in and watched as Jane logged in and then brought up a folder with pictures.

"These were taken early that morning by some skiers that wanted the first powder of the day," Jane explained. "They are waiting for the lift to open when they see a helicopter land on the hotel's helipad."

"That person is quite the photographer," Tammy admired the clear close-up of the helicopter. "What is that emblem on it?"

"I'll get there," Jane assured her. "Look who gets out of it."

"He looks familiar," Tammy's brows drew into a frown.

"He should. He was one of the youngest tech CEOs of his time and his company has just about consumed all its competition as it keeps growing," Jane told her. "That's Jason Brown."

"Jason Brown?" Tammy looked at Jane questioningly. "If that is him..." She stopped and looked at his picture. "He really is quite young, isn't he?"

"He's in his mid to late twenties. No one really knows for sure because he is very close-mouthed about his personal life," Jane explained.

"So why are we so interested in him?" Tammy looked at Jane curiously. "A lot of high-profile people go to the resort by helicopter."

"Yes, but he doesn't stay." Jane clicked off that photo and clicked on the next one. "Fifteen minutes later, he emerges with this woman." She stood back. "Recognize her?"

Tammy froze when she saw Ursula, Martin's girlfriend getting into the chopper with Jason Brown.

"When we spoke on the phone, you mentioned that she had left earlier and was the only one that wasn't there," Jane told Tammy. "I wasn't actually looking for her, and I didn't even know who she was when I saw this photo. In fact, I thought nothing of the photo at all."

"So why are we looking at it now?" Tammy's frown deepened. "And why is Ursula leaving with Jason Brown?" She bit her lip. "Maybe he was going to invest in Martin's new show?"

"Or maybe they were planning an avalanche to solve both their problems at once!" Jane offered some insight.

"Are you trying to say that Jason Brown was somehow responsible for the avalanche?" Tammy looked at Jane, amazed.

"I'm saying he could be," Jane clicked on another photo. "The helicopter didn't leave the resort's vicinity but headed to the mountains."

Tammy saw another photo of a helicopter hovering at the top of the mountains.

"That could be any helicopter," Tammy told her.

"No." Jane shook her head. "Here, look at this picture. The skiers were closer to the top of the mountain when this one was taken. The emblem you asked me about is Jason's company emblem on his helicopter."

"Oh!" Tammy felt little shocks tingle through her fingertips when she saw the next picture.

The helicopter was suspended, and someone hung from a ladder, dropping something into the snow.

"What is that?" Tammy asked, squinting in on the objects.

"My brother believes they are explosive devices," Jane told her. "There's more."

"Wait, does your father have these photos?" Tammy asked her.

"Yes." Jane nodded. "He got them from my brother, who was helping me blow the pictures up so we could see more detail in them."

"He couldn't have been pleased about that." Tammy looked at Jane.

"No, he wasn't," Jane told her and put her hand on the folder. "I copied some of his files on the case. They have been investigating it for over six months now."

"Why?" Tammy asked.

"The owners wanted a quiet investigation into what happened because this now impacts their nearly perfect safety record," Jane explained. "One of the resort's many snow cameras surveying the mountains picked up almost the same picture before it died."

"So, it wasn't an accident?" Tammy swallowed as the emotions started to rise in her stomach once again.

"It seems Jason had a few people he thought he could get rid of all at once," Jane told her. "Your husband got an invitation to the ski resort, as did your brother. Your brother was looking for investors to help the ranches while Martin was looking for them for his TV show."

"So, Martin wasn't after my brother to invest?" Tammy frowned, confused. "I thought Ursula said..."

"I don't think you can rely on what she told you," Jane pointed out. "It seems Ursula had been in contact with Jason for a good few months before the accident. My brother found multiple exchanges through emails and some other dark website between them."

"Does your brother work for the FBI?" Tammy asked.

"No, he what they call a white hat." Jane smiled as Tammy's eyes widened in surprise. "He and I both consult from time to time for the FBI though."

"Nice," Tammy said. "I think Jason wanted to get rid of your brother and Ursula wanted to cash in on Martin's money."

"But a lot of other people were killed and badly injured that day as well," Tammy said. "That was a bit drastic, wasn't it?"

"Here is a list of all those that were killed." Jane clicked on a PDF document and turned it in for Tammy to see. "Do you recognize any other names?"

"No!" Tammy's eyes widened. "Two are rival tech companies, and is that Carlos Santiago?" She looked at Jane, shocked. "Carlos is dead?"

"He too received an invite with a baited hook about a potential investor wanting to invest in his TV network, which was also in a bit of trouble at the time," Jane told her.

"Uncle Robert and I always suspected that Carlos was the real father of Ursula's baby," Tammy told her.

"He was." Jane opened another document. "This is the paternity test that Carlos had just ordered Ursula to take."

"So, she had Martin and Carlos killed?" Tammy couldn't believe what she was hearing.

"I think so." Jane clicked on another document. "Here are some messages between her and Jason. He promises her both networks, the one Martin used to own and Carlos'."

"Wow!" That was all Tammy could say. How cold-blooded was that woman? "I just gave her son a trust fund and bought her a house."

"Which she was not very happy about. She wanted all your houses and most of your money that she insists you took from your ex-husband." Jane showed her another email. "In fact, Jason told her not to worry. He could get her a whole lot more and make sure you paid."

"Paid for what exactly?" Tammy asked. "I've done nothing to Ursula. She was the one who destroyed my marriage."

"I don't think she's the only one that wants to make you pay." Jane's voice dropped. "I'm sorry, Tammy, but, for some reason, Jason Brown has it out for you."

"What?" Tammy hissed. "I don't understand. I don't even know him."

"He knows you and everyone else in Lewistown that he's coming after." Jane looked at her worriedly. "Tammy, my brother and I think Jason Brown is behind all this trouble."

"Why?" Tammy was confused. "Does he want our land?"

"I'd say that and revenge." Jane clicked on some more photos. "He's had these guys, who we managed to find out work for him, following you, Cat, Chelsea, Ashley, and Maria for months."

"Why, though?" Tammy asked again, completely baffled as to why Jason Brown wanted revenge on them.

"I'm sorry, but that is something my brother and I don't know," Jane told her.

"Then maybe we can figure this all out together." Wallace's deep soft voice made them jump.

Jane and Tammy spun around to see him leaning casually in the doorway.

"Your presence is being missed." Wallace pushed himself out of the door and walked into the room. "So, Jane, you're a spy during your off hours now?"

"No." Jane's cheeks turned pink. "My father won't let me go into the FBI."

"Well, how about you and your brother come work for me?" Wallace grinned at her wide-eyed look, pulling a business card from his pocket and handing it to Jane. "But you can't let your father or anyone else know. We could use two people like you on our team."

"Who's 'we'?" Jane and Tammy asked him at the same time.

"I can't say now," Wallace told them. "Jane, I think you should stay here and wait for your father to leave." He looked at

Tammy. "You need to come back to the living room to get Jane's father and his partner to go."

"Right!" Tammy said. "I'll be back as soon as I can. You can go to the kitchen. My aunt will get you refreshments while you wait."

"Can I go look at the horses?" Jane asked her.

"Sure, Aunt Molly will take you." Tammy left Jane and followed Wallace back to the living room.

After another fifteen minutes of being warned about the avalanche investigation by Agent Yates and his partner, the two agents eventually left.

"Tammy, I know you're mad at me right now," Robert looked at her. "But please, can you and Greg let me in on what the heck is going on?"

"As Greg and I have managed to call a truce and put our difference aside for now," Tammy told her uncle, "I'm willing to do the same with you. We could use all the help we can get right now, especially after what I've just learned."

She looked at Wallace, who nodded and walked off towards the back of the house.

"Come with me." Tammy looked from Robert to Greg. "There's something you both need to see."

✦

Twenty minutes later, Greg sat staring at Jane's computer screen in disbelief. Jason Brown, a hotshot young tech millionaire, was gunning for them.

"Why don't we interrogate that Ursula woman?" Greg asked.

"We can't do that," Wallace shook his head. "We don't want to alert either Jason or her that we're on to them in any way. That will either spook them or make them reckless. Either way, they will up the game whatever it is and probably escalate it."

"It makes no sense." Greg shook his head again. "I can understand Donaldson's construction wanting the land and probably doing all this, but not a tech millionaire. What has he possibly got to gain, and what grudge could he hold against all of us?"

"That, Greg my friend, is what we need to find out." Wallace looked at his watch. "What time is your brother meeting us?" He asked Jane.

"In an hour," Jane told Wallace.

"Then we'd better get going," Wallace told her. "I think it best if you leave your car here and come in mine just in case your father has people watching Double A."

"I wouldn't put it past him," Jane agreed with Wallace.

"Then you'll need to go out wearing my hat and coat, hiding your face," Tammy suggested. "If someone is watching, they'll assume it's me leaving with Wallace."

"Weren't we supposed to be interviewing a new housekeeper about now?" Greg noticed the time.

"I postponed the meeting," Molly told them from the study's doorway. "The girls, Amy, and Jude are back. It is also dinnertime." She looked at Jane and Wallace. "Are you sure you won't stay for dinner?"

"We would love to," Wallace answered for himself and Jane. "But we have another important meeting to get to."

"Fair enough, another time then." Molly gave them both a warm smile. "Dinner is in ten minutes." She left the study.

"That's our cue." Wallace stood and helped Jane gather her things. "We'll touch base again tomorrow." He looked at Tammy, who nodded in confirmation.

Greg and Tammy walked them to the door. They stood side by side in the darkened doorway, watching the car disappear down the drive. They both turned together to walk back inside and didn't realize how close they were until their bodies collided. Greg reached out to steady Tammy, pulling her into his arms. His pulse immediately went wild when their shocked eyes locked and held. Tammy's soft hands were pressed up against Greg's chest, and his arms automatically tightened around her.

"Tammy!" Greg's voice was a hoarse whisper as her name tore from his throat. "I..."

Before he could say another word, their lips met. They melted into each other as they answered the cry of their broken souls and the longing in their wounded hearts. Tammy's hands slid up his chest to lock around the back of his head, drawing them closer together. All the tension brewing between them since their eyes had collided the first day Tammy arrived home spilled into the kiss. The hurt and heartache of their past relationship faded away with the world around them. In that moment, there was only them and the memory of how it had once been between them.

"Uhh hum!" The sound of someone clearing their throats seemed to come from somewhere far away and didn't register until the second time. "I don't mean to interrupt, but your aunt asked me to come to get you for dinner."

Tammy and Greg sprung apart at the sound of Jude's amused voice. Neither of them looked at Jude as they stared at each other in shock.

"I want to walk back the way I came and leave you two alone, because, personally, I think it's about time you two admitted what everyone else already knows," Jude told them. "But, from what I've gathered over the past week, the two of you have a lot of baggage to sort through. So, you'll both hate me and thank me for not leaving right now."

Tammy was the first to snap out of the state of disbelief over what had just happened between them. Her cheeks pinkened, and she spun around, flying past Jude, and nearly knocking the big guy over in her haste to get away. Greg turned to watch her rush up the stairs and knew she was headed for her room.

"I'll take her a tray in a few minutes." Jude gave Greg a small smile before turning and walking off towards the dining room.

Greg took a few minutes to gather himself and calm his overloaded system down. He couldn't believe what he'd just done or even remember who made the first move. Greg's mind was racing as fast as his heart was, and his legs felt like jelly. Every little touch or look he and Tammy had shared over the past few days had sent a jolt through him. From way back when they'd first kissed at her prom, he'd known how potent she was to him. But now that they were older, she was deadly, and Greg knew, without a shadow of a doubt, that it was too late for him. He may have managed to push her from his mind for over thirty years when she was out of sight. But he'd know that, even though Tammy had been ripped from his soul, she had always taken up the biggest part of his heart.

Greg had worried that there was something wrong with him that he couldn't love his wife the way she wanted him to love her. He'd even tried dating a few times, but there had never been anyone special who could ignite that flame in him. Greg knew deep down that he had known the answer as to why. He just never wanted to admit it, but now, he knew he could no longer hide from himself. Tammy was the only one who held the torch that could ignite the flame that would bring his soul to life once again and reopen his heart to love. He pinched the bridge of his nose, trying to get a grip on the turmoil churning inside him. Opening his eyes, Greg looked towards the stairs where Tammy had run. Greg knew if he ever came close to standing a chance of winning Tammy's heart again, they had to go down a very painful memory lane. It would not only cause him pain but also open old wounds for both of them.

"Dad?" Maggie's voice drew him back to reality, and his eyes squinted through the darkening hallway to see her small frame highlighted in the dining-room door.

"Are you coming?" Maggie asked him. "Dinner's getting cold, and Aunt Molly doesn't like to reheat anything in the microwave."

"I'll be there in a minute, honey," Greg assured her with a warm smile.

Maggie nodded and ducked back into the dining room.

Greg glanced at the stairs once more time, took a deep breath, and forced himself to regain control over his churning emotions and deep thoughts before joining the family for dinner. Jude gathered a plate for Tammy, informing the family that she'd come down with a headache, and apologized for not being at dinner. Greg was about to offer to take the plate to her but thought better of it when Jude threw him a look. The look said Jude understood but also warned Greg that now wasn't the time. And as much as Greg wanted to rush into Tammy's room and demand they talk it all through, he knew Jude was right. This time, Greg was going to do it right. He'd wasted nearly an entire lifetime licking his wounds where Tammy was concerned instead of admitting his part in it all. Maybe if he'd done that sooner, he and Tammy would never have lived a life apart.

THE SERIES CONTINUES

ARE YOU READY TO READ Four Lakes Ranch, book 5 of the Montana Country Inn Romance Series?

To read the next book in this series, go to www.amazon.com/dp/B0B6DN4TVT

ALSO BY AMY RAFFERTY

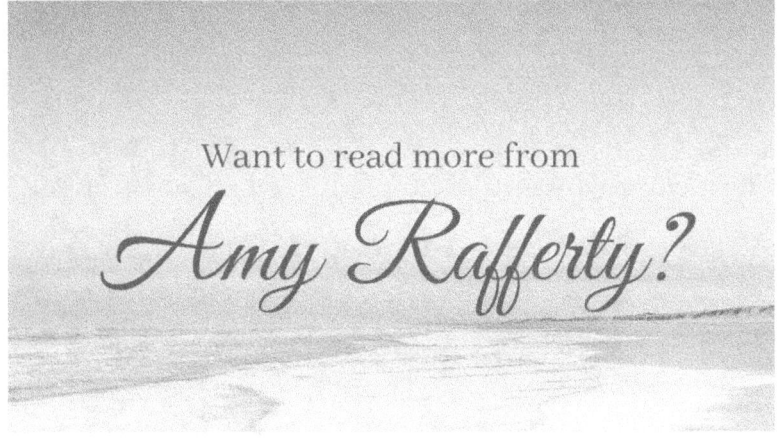

To dive into your next read, go to https://www.amyraffertyauthor.com/

STAY UPDATED WITH ME

Thank you so much for purchasing or downloading my book! I am grateful to all my amazing readers.

To stay updated on all my latest books, newsletters, freebies and beautiful photos from the fabulous locations I write about, why not join my VIP group?

I will send you regular pictures of La Jolla Cove, San Diego and the Florida Gulf Beaches where I try to spend as much time as I can. I live in San Diego, my own 'Garden Of Eden' and I am in love with the sea and the beaches in the area. They inspire me to write lots of beachy mystery romance fiction to share with my awesome readers like you. To join me go to https://landing.mailerlite.com/webforms/landing/y6w2d2

You will be asked for your email. You also get a FREE BOOK whenever you sign-up!

FREE BOOK

To get your FREE copy of Cody Bay Inn Prequel - Nantucket Calling go to www.amazon.com/B0992NFTY1

ABOUT THE AUTHOR

Amazon #1 Best-Seller, Amy Rafferty is a contemporary romance author of feel-good beach romance reads with heartwarming stories embracing humor and love.

Born in New York, previously a Lawyer, she now lives in San Diego with her beautiful children and cats!

Aside from writing, publishing and running her home, she spends as much time as she can visiting the beautiful San Diego and Florida beaches where she has family and friends. She calls San Diego her 'Garden of Eden', inspiring her to write clean and wholesome romance novels incorporating mystery, suspense and adventures for her characters as they find a way to open their hearts and let true love in.

facebook.com/amyraffertyauthor
instagram.com/amyraffertyauthor

www.ingramcontent.com/pod-product-compliance
Lightning Source LLC
LaVergne TN
LVHW021815060526
838201LV00058B/3402